The Bean Store

Book One

The Map of Eternity

Other Fiction by Warren Firschein:

The Pirate of Janaconda Island (2017)

Out of Synch (2015)

The Bean Store

Book One

The Map of Eternity

Warren Firschein

CHAPTER TWO PRESS ◇ SAFETY HARBOR, FL

THE BEAN STORE:
THE MAP OF ETERNITY

For you, you,
and especially *you*.

PART ONE

CHAPTER 1

Summer Vacation

Jules sat at his desk thinking, as he often did, about the sea.

From his seat in the last row, he watched the colorful fish darting around in the classroom aquarium, propped up on a cabinet near the windows. The sunlight sliced through the tank at a crooked angle, causing the tiny particles in the water to sparkle as if they were fluorescent. He was busy imagining what it would be like to swim along the bottom of the ocean like an eel or mermaid when, without warning, the serenity was shattered by the sudden *clang* of the school bell.

A shout of joy rang out as the students collected their things and scurried toward the door, toward the sunshine and beyond.

"Remember, children," shouted Ms. Binkley, trying to maintain both her dignity and her composure in the midst of all the chaos, accomplishing neither. "When you return in the fall, each of you must submit a twenty-page report on what you did during your summer vacation. Twenty pages, mind you, and not a single one less."

But the children hardly heard her. They had endured nine long months of arithmetic problems and science experiments, not to mention the endless reading assignments and spelling tests, and now, finally, they were free of such nonsense until September. Shouting with glee, they scampered out into the warm, humid air, talking excitedly about their plans for the summer.

"I'm going to a horse camp," Elmira Eldritch boasted to a group of girls that were clustered around her. She was a tall, gangly girl with a pointy nose that turned up slightly at its tip, who liked to be the center of attention. "I'll be there for eight whole weeks. My Mom says I'll learn to ride horses and get them to jump over fences and stuff like that." She brushed her bangs out of her eyes with a flourish like a movie star. "I can't wait."

"Oh, that sounds *wonderful*," Matilda Flupnik chimed in as she twirled her copper hair with her index finger, although her tone indicated a very different opinion. "I wish I could go to your little farm too, but *naturally* I'm going to be in Spain with my family. Did you know," she continued, "that horses were originally brought here from Spain? Perhaps my father will let me ride one while I'm there. I'm sure I'll be an expert rider in no time. I once rode a llama at a zoo; I'm sure it couldn't be much different."

The other girls groaned quietly. Matilda considered herself an expert on Spain and was always going on and on about what things were like there. Her grandmother lived in Barcelona, and every summer she'd go visit. Last fall she returned with tales about castles high up on mountaintops and charcoal-colored bulls that slept in flower beds along the side of the road. The girls hardly knew whether to believe her or not, but despite their skepticism, they all felt a pang of jealousy when Matilda mentioned her annual trip, as they did each fall when she described her adventures.

Then the awkward moment passed and everyone started talking at once, bragging about their upcoming camps and vacations, trying to make them sound as exciting as Elmira's and Matilda's. One boy said he was going to a resort on a remote Caribbean island for a week, while another was going hiking in the desert with his family. Their voices wove together with those of groups of children from other classes performing similar end-of-year rituals, forming a discordant jumble of noise. Jules, listening from inside the school through a cracked window, could barely tell them apart. After a few minutes, the children tired of this game, said their goodbyes and see-you-laters, and drifted off toward their homes. The voices dwindled away.

When it sounded as though everyone had gone, he left the spot where he'd been hiding and trudged slowly toward the door. Like most of his class, he was ten years old, although he was small for his age. A swollen book bag was slung over one shoulder. His head hung, and with his chin nearly touching his chest, it was a wonder he could see where he was going. Had he not known every turn in the winding corridors by heart, he surely would have bumped his head into a wall or doorway or even a locker on his way out of the school. All he could see were his shoes, a ratty pair of old sneakers that were almost completely brown with grime.

He stepped out into the sunlight, blinked twice, and began to run, hoping no one would notice him. He hadn't taken more than three steps before the toe of his shoe caught on the edge of a concrete slab and he tumbled forward, landing on his knees and scraping his palms on the dirt.

"Here, let me help you up, Jules," said Ms. Binkley, who had exited the school just after him. "You're not hurt, are you?" She reached out and tugged on his elbow until he had gotten on his feet again. "Maybe we should let the nurse look at you before you go home. I think she's still here."

Jules looked away and pulled his arm back, shaking his head just enough so he was sure she had seen it.

"What's the matter?" his teacher asked, frowning. "Aren't you looking forward to your vacation like the others?"

Jules barely shrugged his shoulders and didn't answer. The truth was, unlike the other kids in the class, he didn't have any special summer plans to get excited about. As a matter of fact, he had hidden in the bathroom until they had all left so he wouldn't have to listen to the unending descriptions of their upcoming family trips and camps and face the embarrassment of standing by silently. Last year, on the final day of school, he'd made the mistake of running out of the classroom along with the others, only to be ridiculed when he told them what he'd be doing for the summer. He wouldn't go through that again! So this year, he waited in the bathroom until he thought it was safe to leave the school. But for some reason, though, that didn't make him feel any better.

"Well, then, have a good vacation, Jules," Ms. Binkley said after the lengthy silence had begun to become uncomfortable. "I'll see you in September. And don't forget the report. What you did during the summer. Remember, Jules, *twenty pages*. It's due your first day back in the fall. You'll have to start several weeks ahead to get it finished in time. We wouldn't want a repeat of last year's fiasco, now, would we?"

Jules felt his face get warm at the memory. "No, ma'am," he said, wondering why he had to have the same teacher three years in a row. He was pretty sure that the other teachers didn't ever assign summer writing assignments, so why did she? "Have a nice summer, Miss Binkley," he mumbled, and set off toward home.

Why *wouldn't* he remember last summer's book report? It was a complete disaster. Yet even now, nine months later, Ms. Binkley misjudged the effort he had put into it. Knowing how difficult and time-consuming it was for him to read, Jules hadn't waited until the last minute to begin; no, she was wrong about that. In fact, he had finished reading his chosen book, *The*

Puppeteer of Perth, well before the end of July, leaving plenty of time for the writing. He had such grand plans for his paper, too. He intended to compare his own life to the troubles faced by the puppeteer in the story. It would be both funny and sad at the same time, like true stories often are. He imagined Ms. Binkley reading the report aloud to the class, and the polite applause and the expressions of admiration on the faces of his classmates when she finished. Elmira would exclaim that it was "the best report she had ever heard," and wipe the tears from her eyes.

But, alas, his mind remained blank. For hours on end he sat on the floor in front of the old, oversized bean crate he often used as a desk, staring emptily into space, at small nail-holes in the far wall or perhaps at some stains on the ceiling, searching for inspiration, but nothing would come to him. By the time the candles had gone out, all he ever managed to create were drawings on the floor with shards of coal from the furnace, eventually going to sleep without writing a single word. His favorite effort was a sketch of a giant rabbit with big black fangs chasing Ms. Binkley through a field. The next morning, his mother trembled with rage and made him mop away the mess before a customer came in and saw his artwork.

Finally, when the start of the school year was only days away, Jules realized he couldn't put it off any more. With a sigh of resignation, he reached for his pencil, only to discover that a mouse had gnawed it down while he was busy daydreaming over the past several weeks. Now it was useless, a stub of splintered wood no longer than his thumb. Annoyed at his inattentiveness, his mother refused to provide him with another. "Pencils don't grow on trees," she had said, her hands planted resolutely on her hips. "You must learn to be more responsible for your things." She had even suggested, condescendingly, that he write the report with coal from the furnace and illustrate it with drawings of ferocious jackrabbits.

Panic!

Then, in a flash of inspiration, Jules remembered his childhood crayon collection, and sure enough, he found it deep inside the old toy chest, now covered with dust and cobwebs. Personally, he thought it was a pretty clever idea to write each paragraph in a different color; that way, he could claim that he used the crayons on purpose and wouldn't have to explain why he didn't use a pencil like a normal person. But when Ms. Binkley held it up so the other students could see it in all its colorful glory, they laughed so hard that their faces turned red.

"Why is it only eight pages long?" she asked, once the laughter subsided. When he didn't respond, Ms. Binkley asked again, this time more sternly. "*Jules!* Pay attention! Tell me, and tell your classmates too, they deserve to know why your report isn't as long as theirs. Why is it only eight pages long?"

"I ran out of crayons," Jules answered with a shrug, as if the answer should have been obvious to everyone.

Oh, how they howled at *that*. Elmira Eldritch laughed so hard she fell off her chair, which led to more screaming. "Children! Please!" Ms. Binkley exclaimed. "It's not nice to laugh at Elmira." What this meant was: it was okay to laugh at Jules.

And Jules spent the remainder of the school day sitting in the corner, "where he wouldn't disrupt the rest of the class."

No, unlike his classmates, he was definitely, positively *not* looking forward to his summer vacation. Just as with every other summer since he could remember, his days would be spent performing chores in the family store, The Beanery. Mostly they sold coffee beans, but there were also selections of lima beans, Mexican jumping beans, bean sprouts, black beans, refried beans, and green beans. They even sold beanbags, because they fit with the general theme. If it involved beans, they sold it— other than jellybeans, which his father had always believed were good for nothing but rotting children's teeth. So the jellybeans stayed out, and the horrible smell of coffee stank up the air and got in Jules's clothes, hair, and nostrils.

On top of the smell, The Beanery was dark and cramped. There were only two small windows, positioned high on opposite walls near the ceiling. His father originally planned it that way because he thought that too much light would ruin the flavor of the beans. To Jules, though, it felt like a jail.

But even spending all day with his eyes straining against the near-darkness couldn't dull Jules's vibrant imagination. He envisioned his eyeballs growing larger and larger in order to see proper, until they bulged out of his head like those of the cave frogs he had learned about in science class, before finally popping out from behind his eyelids and bouncing across the wooden floor. This notion so terrified him that before bedtime he would stand in front of the bathroom mirror and check their progress, but as far as he could tell they seemed to remain normal size. Of course, his parents didn't fret over the lack of light. They rarely spent time in the store itself, coming in only when the tinkling of the brass doorbells announced the entrance of a potential customer. The rest of the day they'd be in back, where there were plenty of windows, ordering more beans and doing the accounting.

Continuing his long trek home, Jules crossed a narrow creek and cut across an empty, overgrown field. A large crow balanced on the top of a wooden fence post like a sentry, cackling at him as he passed. A couple of years back, the lot had been cleared of trees to make room for a new housing development which was never started, leaving a big blank spot in the landscape as if a giant void had been carved into the earth. To Jules it often felt as if his family lived in the middle of nowhere. He wished they lived close to the center of town, where there were shops and playgrounds and plenty of things to occupy his time. Years ago, his father had picked a spot for the family business out near the edge of the forest, thinking that the town would grow and the area would someday be packed with other stores and houses. But the town hadn't gotten any bigger at all. In fact, during the past few years, six of their neighbors had moved away. A couple of homes were still vacant and remained uncared for, rotting away.

One of these was the old Klepner house, which was a little more than a mile away. Occasionally, when Jules had nothing to do, he'd go and stand near the bushes and peer through the plate-glass living room window, trying to make sense of the odd shadows that seemed to move as he watched and attempt to decipher the faint scratchings and scrapings he heard from within the old walls. Sometimes he considered sneaking in to look around and find out what made those strange noises, but the thought terrified him. The place was probably haunted. Still, he went there sometimes and threw stones at the second-floor windows, but never tried to enter.

He often wondered what his father would think of the weird things he thought he noticed inside the Klepner house, but he'd never find out, not anymore, because now his father was dead. It had happened suddenly, at least suddenly from Jules's perspective, who hadn't known his father was sick at all. That was two full years ago, and Jules still got a knot in his stomach just thinking about it. Since then, he could hardly ever remember his mother laughing or even smiling at him even once. She'd just look at him and say, "That's nice, Jules," whenever he spoke to her. Not as much *at* him as *through* him, as if he wasn't even there at all, her eyes focusing on something far away in place or time, something that only she could see in her mind. "I got a B minus on my reading this week," he said proudly a few months ago. "That's nice, Jules," she replied. "Have you swept the floor of the bean store yet? You must do that before dinner." More often: "Miss Binkley said I am holding the others back, so she made me sit in the corner." "That's nice dear," she'd say with a glazed look. "Have you polished the bean counter? You must do that tonight; we may get a big customer tomorrow."

Yes, it would be another boring summer just like all the others. *It's not that I don't like working in the bean store,* Jules concluded miserably as he turned down the driveway. *It's just that there are so many more interesting things to do.*

He paused. *If only I knew what they were.*

If only.

Jules pulled open the front door, setting off the bells. The store was empty and quiet. The displays were meticulously neat and well organized, and it looked as if there hadn't been a customer all day. He entered and let the door shut behind him.

"I'll be with you in a moment," his mother called from the back in her odd accent. "The shopping baskets are in the corner."

"It's just me," he answered.

Jules crossed the floor and through the door behind the counter, into the living space attached to the store. He dropped his backpack in a corner and continued into the kitchen, where he found his mother hovering over the stove, stirring a pot of stew.

"You'll never believe what I found on the way home from school," he started. "A huge colony of ants, down by that empty field along the road, near the construction site. There must've been thousands of them. They're so funny to watch, the way they're always in a rush to do the same thing as all the others. I was wondering what they might say if they could talk."

"Is that what took you so long getting home?"

"No. I mean, I came right home. I just stopped for a minute to look at them."

"I know that's not true. Probably standing around gabbing with the other children. Really, Jules, you must stop being a laggard. Why, I heard Betsy Bottomsley run past some twelve minutes ago. And she's only in the second grade." The Bottomsleys lived a quarter mile up the road, in the opposite direction from the old Klepner house.

"Third grade now," Jules corrected. "She just graduated."

"It doesn't matter. I don't know how many more times I have to tell you how important it is that you come home right away after school. I can't run this store by myself." She reached out a hand and steadied herself with the edge of the stove. "Not anymore. At least school is out for the summer. Can I rely on you to help out for the next few months?"

Jules nodded.

"Good." She grabbed the large wooden spoon and continued stirring. "It's not that I don't trust you. It's just that you have a tendency to let your mind wander and lose track of time. Do you understand what I'm saying?"

"I think so."

"I'm not against you having a healthy imagination. Goodness knows, your father was much the same way. But you're going to have to learn to focus more on reality instead of making up stories in your head all the time or studying ants. There's a time and place for everything. And I'm afraid things are going to be this way for a while. I don't know what we're going to do when school starts up again in the fall. We're going to have to think of something."

She paused before continuing. "Perhaps you and Betsy should walk home together after school next year. That would almost guarantee that you'd come straight home without delay and won't waste as much time. I should speak to Betsy's mother and arrange it. Yes, this is what I will do." She waved the large wooden spoon in the air to punctuate her words. Little bits of stew flew through the air, making a mess on the floor. The kitchen walls were flaked with faded brown stains, evidence of previous conversations that had gone much the same way. "I think that would work out splendidly. You should spend more time with that Bottomsley girl anyway," she said, nodding her head sharply. "Maybe even starting this summer. She'll teach you about responsibility."

Jules sighed; his shoulders slumped forward. "Betsy? Really, Mom," he said, "nobody likes her. She pinches people."

"Betsy is older now, and I expect that she will stop pinching soon enough, if she hasn't already."

"She smells funny, too. She wears garlic on a string around her neck. I think it's to keep vampires away."

"Vampires? Really, Jules. What a ridiculous suggestion. She wears that garlic to keep from getting sick, which is all the more reason why you should spend time with her. If you stick close to her, maybe you won't get sick yourself. Save me an arm and a leg, it will. Why, if you have to get your tonsils out again, I don't know how we'll pay for it."

She stirred one more time before covering the pot. "We can discuss this further later. Now that you're finally here, I have a few things for you to do in the store that have to be done this evening." She looked at him with her deep bronze-colored eyes, the light glinting against the purple stone hanging from her golden necklace.

"Can't I start tomorrow instead? I mean, it's the first day of summer. I was hoping to go explore some more of the woods."

"I'm sorry. This has to be done, and I can't do it. I think I'm about to have one of my spells." She steadied herself again. "Maybe over the weekend there will be time for you to spend some time by yourself."

As Jules groaned, she motioned for him to follow. She walked almost stiff legged, with a slight hunch in her back, like an old woman who had misplaced her cane. She was only forty-three, but there are ways to measure age other than by years.

After passing through the back door that led into the store, Jules's mother shuffled to a darkened corner and grabbed a large vat that was filled with coffee beans. She struggled with its weight, but still managed to drag it to the center of the room, next to an old straw broom she had used to sweep up before Jules had returned home from school.

"The store hasn't been doing too well recently," she started. "You know that. I've been trying to save money wherever we can until business picks up. Every little bit helps. Anyway, McAllister, who we buy coffee beans from, offered to sell us his remainder at a huge discount."

"Remainder? What's that?"

"The leftover coffee beans he was unable to sell. He gets a new shipment from the wholesaler every few weeks, and he usually just throws away what's left from the prior batch. He does a good job controlling his inventory, so it usually doesn't amount to very much, but it's more than enough for our small store for a few weeks. The problem is that in order to fill an entire barrel, he had to mix all the different flavors together. We can't sell them that way. No one wants to drink a cup of coffee that is partly one flavor and partly a completely different one. So you'll have to separate them again so we can sell them. If you don't procrastinate, you should be finished soon enough."

"But—they all look alike!" Jules complained.

"I'm quite aware of that. It seems that you won't need new glasses this year after all. You'll have to use your sense of smell instead." Reaching into the vat, she picked up a single brown coffee bean and shoved it halfway up her left nostril. "Ahhhh, amaretto," she said after a deep inhalation. She removed the bean and placed in on the floor, all by itself. "There! I've gotten you started on the amaretto pile."

She shut her eyes and started to wobble. "I should go lie down now. I'll leave a bowl of stew outside the door for when you get hungry. Please be careful not to step on any of the mouse traps." With that, she lit two large candles, placed them strategically on the floor, and went out the back door, leaving Jules alone to his thoughts.

CHAPTER 2

An Odd Visitor

The white tallow candles flickered in the darkness, casting menacing shadows across the floor and the walls. Jules picked up the first bean and stared at it.

"She's crazy if she thinks I'm going to stick this up my nose," he mumbled. "That's disgusting."

He studied the small bean from a distance, trying to identify it from its shape and color. He held it by its ends with his thumb and forefinger, turning it from side to side to catch the light at the best angle. When that failed, he brought it as close to his nostril as he dared and sniffed hard. Unsure, he placed it next to the amaretto bean and picked up another, and then another.

Time passed. Jules gradually improved his skill at identifying the different aromas, and his movements acquired a distinct rhythm. Other than the sound of Jules sniffing each coffee bean and placing it in its correct pile, the store was eerily quiet. Jules's mother had gone to bed hours earlier, without even wishing him goodnight.

Jules and his mother lived in a few sparse rooms connected to the rear of the store. The house was originally designed to accommodate a small business in the front, and so the living area was accessible through the door behind The Beanery's counter, as well as by a wooden porch attached to the kitchen. One of the bedrooms had been converted into an office, so Jules slept in what used to be a large utility closet that didn't have any windows. Despite the lack of light, he didn't mind so much. There was enough room for a few dressers and to stretch out on the floor in his sleeping bag, and that's all that mattered to him.

The rest of the house was cozy but functional. The living room contained a reclining chair and a sleeper sofa, as well as a wooden table where Jules and his mother ate when guests came over, which was almost never. Along one wall, a large bookcase overflowed with old novels that had once belonged to Jules's father. All were thrilling tales of adventure, such as stories of young men sailing on the high sea and of long quests to fulfill some important destiny. Often Jules pulled them from the shelves and ran his fingers over the covers and bent corners, thinking about his father, but he didn't dare try to read them himself, in part because he found it frustrating to work out all the words. Instead, he replayed them in his mind, in his father's deep, soothing voice, often wondering what it would be like if he were involved in a great tale like the ones in the books. Even at his age, though, he realized that such adventures were unlikely to ever happen to him, and that his destiny undoubtedly was to spend his life tending to the family store. At times, he would have imaginary conversations inside his head with his favorite characters and would even make up his own stories, although he could never write them down; that would take much too long.

Jules sighed and stretched his arms. He watched wax run down one of the candles like a teardrop until it settled on the floor, and he wondered why his mother was so reluctant to use electric lights. Things would be so much easier if they just had some lamps like normal families.

By now his shoulders throbbed and his nostrils ached from all the sniffing. Yet he didn't dare stop his task, for he was nowhere near finished, and his mother told him to finish by morning. Jules groaned with dismay. He had absolutely no idea how many beans he had already sorted. It could have been hundreds; it could have been thousands. *Perhaps even tens of thousands.* Five little piles had slowly grown into grapefruit-sized mounds at his feet.

Then Jules heard a faint scratching sound. Looking up, he caught a glimpse of a small critter scurrying across the floor.

There's that mouse, he gasped. For nine long months he had searched the store for the mouse that gnawed away his only pencil and caused his embarrassment on the first day of school.

For nine long months, he had looked for holes in the walls and gaps in the baseboards, and left traps in the corners to catch the thing. Yet for nine long months, he had come up empty. Now, with revenge throbbing through his veins, he grabbed the broom and wielded it like a baseball bat.

"Where are you? Where did you go?" he called out. Jules gripped the handle until his knuckles turned white and his palms stung. "Come out, mouse. I won't hurt you," he lied.

The handle felt good in his hands. To him it was no longer a spindly broom, but a fearsome weapon worthy of conquering the most frightful beasts imaginable, and he longed to use it. He took a wild practice swing and accidentally knocked the bean counter onto the floor with a resounding *clang*. Jules scrambled to pick it up and placed it back where it had been, hoping his mother wouldn't notice the dent when she awoke in the morning.

Jules sighed. Surely that ruckus had scared away the mouse. He'd never catch it now. Frustrated, he kicked at the broom and watched it slide across the floor until it came to rest underneath one of the windows. A spider climbed on top of the bristles and began spinning a web.

Not knowing what else to do, Jules reached back into the vat and removed another handful of smelly coffee beans. He held one bean after another up to his left nostril, inhaled deeply until he could identify the scent, and placed each into its correct pile. French roast, cinnamon, French roast. If only he hadn't swung that broom! Sumatra, French roast, amaretto. But he couldn't help it; it made him feel tough, almost invincible.

Then Jules heard another faint scraping noise. He flinched. *Maybe the mouse is still here.*

With single-minded determination, he focused on the barely audible sound in the slim hope that it was just his mother wandering around, but he soon yielded to the inevitable conclusion: the noise was not coming from the kitchen. Either it was from something inside the shop, or he was just imagining things as usual.

Well, he thought, *I'd better stay on the safe side.* If it was a mouse, and the mouse was here in the shop with him, then it probably was none too happy about being chased with a broom and startled by the clank of the falling bean counter. Jules knew that if he were the mouse, he'd be pretty angry, too.

He glanced around in a panic. By now the creature had grown in his imagination to the size of a wild cat, its ferocious jaws lined with two rows of razor-sharp fangs. Jules realized that against such a horrible, dangerous creature, he needed something to defend himself. He looked longingly at the broom lying at the other end of the floor. He could go get it, of course, but that would take time, and what if the mouse managed to attack him first? He needed to act quickly.

Then he saw his mother's old wooden bucket. It was just a few feet away, and he could probably reach it without much effort. The partially-rotted wood slats had narrow gaps between them, but it was probably sturdy enough to smash a mouse with.

Staying on his knees, he slid the short distance across the floor, grabbed the bucket, and returned to his original spot in front of the vat.

Now armed, he decided to practice with this new weapon. Jules held the bucket high over his head, and then flung it downward with a sudden movement, as if trying to crush something against the floor. Something flew out of the bucket and hit him in the face.

"Aaah!" Jules squealed.

It was just a lump of old brown weeds. His mother must have been working in the garden again and neglected to clean up afterwards. Jules sighed; he'd have to get the broom anyway to sweep up the mess before morning, or he'd never hear the end of it. He picked up one of the longer weeds and smelled it cautiously. "Onion," he murmured, wrinkling his nose.

Something else had fallen out besides the decaying onion stalks, too. It was a pair of thick mud-caked gloves that his mother must have been wearing. He put the gloves aside, placed the bucket on the floor next to him, and, after assuring himself that the mouse wasn't nearby, returned to his task of sorting the coffee beans.

Cinnamon, Sumatra, amaretto.

Jules sighed again. The summer was just one evening old, and already he had been sentenced to bean-sorting duty, had dented the bean counter, and had been bombarded by a bucketful of stinky weeds. And to top it off, the stew his mother had left for him had been cold. He ate it right after the sun had set but wished he hadn't. It tasted like cardboard and mashed potatoes, which was not at all like what stew was supposed to taste like. Now his tummy was feeling funny. At first he thought that it could have been due to the excitement of hearing the mouse scurrying about the room, but he was beginning to think it was the effect of the beef stew. Maybe there was never a mouse at all. Maybe the stew was triggering hallucinations. He held the next coffee bean against his left nostril and inhaled deeply.

Hazelnut.

Jules looked around, confused. What had happened to the pile of hazelnut beans? It was now just a small heap of wood shavings.

A tiny creature scampered away in the darkness. It was nothing more than a shadow, and if Jules hadn't been looking up at the critical moment, he wouldn't have noticed it at all. With his instincts taking over, he reached down, picked up the bucket, and lunged toward the shadow.

"Aha!" he cried, dropping the bucket on top of the mouse. "Gotcha! Now, you little scamp, give me back my hazelnut beans!"

Despite Jules's threats and tough talk, he didn't have the heart to hurt the little thing, and at the last moment had decided to capture it under the bucket instead of smashing it and killing it dead. But now he realized the flaw in this decision. If he let the mouse go, of course, it would just return to cause more havoc. Jules sat down in the dust, cross-legged, and pondered his next move.

After some time had passed, it eventually dawned on him that he had yet to hear any sounds from inside the bucket, not even a tiny squeak. Had he missed? It was certainly possible; after all, he wasn't exactly well known for his athletic ability, and could hardly even throw a ball straight. And there was still the chance there was nothing there at all, that he was just suffering from dementia brought on by the spoilt stew. He would have to find out, if for no other reason than to determine whether he was going crazy.

Of course, he couldn't simply lift the bucket and peer underneath. Jules recognized that right away. The mouse—assuming it was under there at all—would simply use the opportunity to run off. So reaching down, he picked up one of the stiffer onion weeds and thrust it through one of the gaps in the slats of the bucket. Immediately he heard a high-pitched squeal, and the weed was yanked out of his hand and pulled inside.

"Well," Jules said out loud. "At least I know that the little fella's in there. Now what should I do with him?"

His mind raced. He could keep it as a pet. Train it to come when he whistled. Bring it to school. Frighten the girls, particularly that smarmy Elmira Eldritch. He could teach it to sneak into *her* home and gnaw away at *her* pencils.

This idea made him giggle. He began to wonder how he would care for the mouse if he did decide to keep it. What did it like to eat?

Maybe it likes beans, Jules thought. He glanced around the room at the displays of lima beans and garbanzo beans and soybeans, until his gaze froze on the pile of wood shavings that had mysteriously replaced the small mound of hazelnut-flavored coffee beans on the floor.

Obviously it likes beans!

Then he realized that in all the excitement he had forgotten about the huge vat of coffee beans still waiting to be sorted. This was just wasting time. With a new anger welling up inside him, he picked up another stiff weed and stabbed it through a gap between two of the pail's slats, over and over.

"Take that, mouse!" he exclaimed as a muted squeal echoed under the bucket. "Serves you right. Making me forget my job. I'll be up all night because of you."

"Okay, you win," a muffled voice called out from beneath the bucket. "Cease and desist yer pokin', mind you. I'll return yer beans."

The hairs on the back of Jules's neck rose up, and his heart hammered in his chest. "Wh—who said that?"

"Who d'yer think?" the voice said again. "The stupid mouse that lives in th' wall? Hoo-boy! For a big person, you sure have 'n awful small brain."

Jules trembled with anger. "Quiet, you!" he exclaimed. "Or I'll—I'll—I'll smack you with the broom, that's what I'll do." But the broom still lay out of reach against the far wall, and he was rooted in his spot with fear.

"Ooh, now there's an idea," said the voice. Clearly, the creature—whatever it was—wasn't the least bit frightened by this threat. "Make sure yer not standin' near anythin' breakable; hate for you to git yer mum after ya." The creature cackled with glee.

Then it chanted:

Swing that broom by the handle.
Watch out for the burning candle!
For if you knock it to the floor
up in flames will go your store.

Swing once!
Swing twice!
Try to miss that counting device!
Shake! Quake!
Big mistake!
Here comes Mum—what did you break?

I ain't afraid to play this game;
'cause I have seen your awful aim.
So swing the broom if you dare
to leave the room in disrepair.

Not very witty perhaps, but all things considered not a bad job, particularly on such short notice. But Jules was not in a proper mood to appreciate poetry, especially a poem that poked fun at him.

"That's ENOUGH!" he cried out. Taunts from his classmates were one thing, but from a mouse trapped beneath a bucket, well, that was quite another!

He pulled on the thick gardening gloves and thrust one hand under the bucket. He sensed the creature darting around, trying as hard as it could to avoid his grasp, but soon enough his hand stumbled on its elusive target. He squeezed. There was another squeal. Through the thick glove, Jules felt the creature squirm and try to wriggle loose. Still, he held on tight. When he thought he had a strong grip on the creature, he very carefully pulled his hand out from under the pail and raised it up to his eye.

Two large eyes peered back at him. Jules stared silently at the creature with rising terror. It wasn't a mouse at all, not even a talking one. His cheeks went numb; his hands shook as a shiver of fright ran down his spine.

Gradually he regained his composure and, without releasing his grip, he began to inspect the creature. He noticed that its head was longer than it was wide, almost egg-shaped, although it was at least three times as big as a goose egg. At the top was a small tuft of thick black hair, which stuck up in a disorderly fashion like a clump of crabgrass. The hair at the left side of the clump was slightly longer than the right end, as though the creature had tried to cut its own hair and wasn't holding the scissors quite straight.

Slightly below and centered between its coal-black eyes was an enormous nose. The nose was the creature's most prominent feature; in fact, that is how Jules recognized that this was no mouse, at least like no mouse that he'd ever seen before. For while mice have large noses, they tend to be narrow and pointy with a few light-colored whiskers affixed to the end. *This* nose was wide and bulbous, with two great nostrils that were as wide around as the creature's eyes, and a large, brownish wart on one side.

Jules couldn't see much more of the creature, for his gloved hand was still gripping it around its midsection. Below his squeezing fingers, though, two enormous, calloused feet stuck out. They were nearly as big as its head was long, and the tops of the toes were hairy. The creature smelled like roasted acorns and damp leaves.

"Wh—what are you?" Jules stammered. When there was no response, he brought his other hand close and pinched the nose hard.

There was a muffled roar of surprise.

"What was that?" Jules asked mischievously. "Don't you have anything else to say? Or are you finished talking?" He pinched one of the largest toes, which curled up almost immediately.

There was another muffled cry. "Oh, right," Jules said. "I'm such an idiot." He shifted his hand until the creature's mouth was uncovered.

The little creature inhaled deeply. "Have ya had yer fun now?" it asked. "Put me down, boy. I'm not a plaything." And with that, it bit down hard on Jules's nearest finger.

"Ow!" Jules shrieked. Instinctively he opened his hand and shook it twice, trying to reduce the sting. The creature fell to the ground, landing hard on its bottom. It got up quickly and stood there, motionless. Jules glared at it. The creature wore a shirt constructed from brown burlap. Below one arm, in faded black print, the shirt read 'McAllister's Grade D Beans.' It was a remnant of one of the burlap bags that the coffee beans were often delivered in.

Obviously, this creature had been here before!

It then turned its back to Jules and walked stiffly toward the bucket. Jules now noticed that it had a tail, a short one, which dragged along the ground as it walked. It placed its hands under the rim of the pail, and with a hearty "heave, ho," flung it aside. Underneath was a small burlap sack, made from another scrap from one of McAllister's bags. The creature walked over to the sack, picked it up, and tossed it in Jules's general direction.

"Here's yer stinkin' beans," it said, and began to walk off. It favored one leg, no doubt a result of being dropped on the ground just moments before.

"Wait!" Jules cried. "What are you? Are you a Leprechaun?"

The creature turned. "I'm a troll, of course, you foolish boy."

Now that it seemed as though the little creature wasn't going to harm him, Jules began to feel sorry for it. He had begun to notice that the burlap shirt had tiny holes in it, and the tuft of hair at the end of its tail was disheveled and tangled with burrs. He opened the burlap sack and spilled some of its contents across the floor.

"Here, you can have some of the beans," he said. "Just don't eat all of them, okay? If I don't have a decent pile of hazelnut beans by tomorrow morning, my mother will think I buried them or ate them or something."

The troll looked back at Jules skeptically, as if it wasn't sure whether Jules was playing a trick that would end with it being trapped under the bucket once again. Then, apparently concluding that Jules was sincere, it nodded its head twice and limped back toward the hazelnut-flavored coffee beans scattered across the floor. Picking up a particularly large bean, the troll began to nibble, although Jules noticed that it made sure to always keep one eye trained on him, just in case.

"I thought trolls were big ugly things that live in caves," Jules said after he could no longer tolerate the silence. "Like ogres. Elmira says that when trolls get tired, they can remove their heads and carry them under their arms. She said she read it in some book."

The little troll didn't look up. "Many different types of trolls," it said between bites, as bits of hazelnut bean sprayed across Jules's sneakers. "Cave trolls, river trolls, mountain trolls." It took another bite. "That particular type of troll yer friend was babblin' about is very special. We call it a *fictional* troll." It took three steps toward Jules and jumped up on his left foot. "There ain't no such thing as a troll that can take off 'is 'ead," it said sternly. "That's just ridiculous. Next thing you'll be tellin' me is that trolls are afraid of goats, too." The troll took one final bite, licked its fingers one by one, and then jumped back down off Jules's foot and greedily picked up another of the hazelnut-flavored beans.

"Well, Elmira said—"

"That Eldritch girl is full of nothin' but nonsense," the little creature interrupted. "Shouldn't be surprised, though. There ain't been no wisdom in none of her family for generations." It reached down, picked up three more coffee beans, and slid them into a previously hidden pocket. Then it stood up as straight as it could, perhaps seven inches tall.

And said: "*I* am a woodland troll. Bergen's my name."

With that, the troll scampered off and disappeared without a trace.

"Well!" said Jules, who didn't even notice which direction the troll had run. "I guess his leg wasn't injured at all like he made it out to be."

For a long minute Jules gazed around the room, staring down low at the baseboards in the hope of catching another glimpse of the creature, but it was useless: the troll was long gone by now, he realized, and there was no point in looking for him in the corners or under the counter. And so with a sigh, Jules sat down in front of the vat, and returned to sorting beans.

CHAPTER 3

Unexpected Freedom

"Just *what* do you think you're doing?"

Jules opened his eyes and looked up to find his mother standing over him, hands planted firmly on her hips.

"Sleeping in the store like a common, well, I don't know what," his mother continued. She reached down and started to pull him to his feet by one of his elbows.

"I'm sorry, I'm sorry," Jules heard himself whimpering. "I must have dozed off while sorting the beans." This was the moment he had dreaded. He had separated and organized the coffee beans until the candles burned out, but had not even begun to make a visible dent in the large vat. He didn't know when he had fallen asleep, but he remembered seeing the moon shining through the western window, so it had to have been just a few hours before dawn.

"I did as much as I could, I'll finish it today," he wanted to say. And he meant it, too, even if he had to go without breakfast. But what he *actually* said was: "I did as—"

For it was at that point he realized his mother had loosened her grip on his arm and wasn't listening to him at all. It was then that he looked around and first noticed the five huge piles of beans neatly arranged in a straight line across the floor. He sneaked a peek into the vat and saw it was empty.

His mother's arms fell to her sides. She opened her mouth as if she intended to say something, but no sound came out. Quite clearly, she had never expected him to complete the task in just one night.

Jules wasn't certain how all the beans got sorted, but he had a pretty good idea. Without missing a beat, he continued, ". . . you asked me to."

"What was that, dear?" said his mother, fingering the purple stone that hung around her neck. She couldn't take her bronze-colored eyes off the piles.

"I did as you asked me to," Jules repeated, quicker this time. "That is, I sorted all the beans."

She mumbled something incoherent.

He pointed confidently at the floor. "Cinnamon, French Roast, amaretto, Sumatra, and the last pile, I believe, are the hazelnut beans."

Jules's mother just nodded. Up and down, up and down. Like her head was attached to a spring.

Jules stood up as straight as an arrow—just like his unusual visitor had done the night before—and announced, "If there isn't anything else, I think I'll just go."

His mother was still too startled to answer. She kept staring at the mounds of beans near her feet, her head rhythmically bobbing up and down.

"Hmmm?" she said at last, just when Jules began to suspect that she had suffered a permanent mental injury. "Yes, yes, of course you are." She waved her hand dismissively without taking her gaze off the floor.

Interpreting that as a positive response, Jules darted out the door, leaving the brass bells tinkling behind him. "I'll be home for dinner," he cried over his shoulder.

An entire day of freedom! What an unexpected treat! But today would not be spent at fun and games. No, he had some serious business to attend to. He ran as fast as he could toward town, his brown hair flapping behind him in the breeze.

Jules was heading for the town library. Prior to the strange events of the previous night and this morning, he would never have imagined that he would go *there*. He certainly wasn't the studious type, and everyone knew it. But Jules needed to do some serious research, and, from what he had heard, the library was just the place for it. More specifically, he was going to the library to learn about trolls. He thought this was a most prudent course of action, especially if that same troll came back, which he thought quite likely. Where did they live? What did they eat? How many were there? And, most importantly (at least from his current point of view), *were they dangerous?* Elmira had said she learned about trolls in a book, didn't she? The troll last night had laughed at what she had told Jules about them, but maybe she read the book wrong, or maybe there was another book. A better book.

Upon arriving all out of breath, Jules marched up the marble steps and passed through the ornate doorway. Once inside, he was immediately awed at the number of shelves. He had never been inside the town library before, and, until now, he never considered that it might be a daunting task to find the particular book he wanted. But there were racks and racks completely full of books. How would he ever find the right one?

He must have had a confused look on his face, for not more than a moment had passed before a tall, thin woman appeared out of nowhere. She wore a dark skirt that hugged her legs, and her silver hair was tied up in a bun so tightly that Jules wondered if it affected her breathing. The woman peered through her glasses and in a pleasant voice asked, "May I assist you, young man?"

"YES!" Jules shouted. "I'd like a book about trolls, please."

The woman made a humming sound from deep within her throat. "Wait here," she said, this time not so pleasantly. "Don't touch anything." She disappeared for a few minutes, and then returned carrying a large book with a hard cover. "Here is one with colorful pictures and big print," she said, speaking as if he was six years old. "Do be careful not to get chocolate on the pages, now that's a good boy." She started off before Jules could thank her.

Jules took a good long look at the book's cover. Across the top, the word 'Trolls' was written in large fanciful script. And, just below that, 'Their Habits and History, written by Frances Farrabee.' At first glance, this certainly seemed like it could be the right book.

Then he noticed the picture underneath the title. It was an illustration of a giant troll marching across the countryside. Anger flashed in its eyes as it crushed trees and bushes with its every step. Jules looked closer and concluded that it wasn't anger in its eyes, but fear. The troll was being chased by a tiny goat, nearly hidden behind the author's name.

"Excuse me," he called after the woman. She stopped and slowly turned to face him. Everyone in the library looked up to see what the ruckus was about. Jules felt his cheeks go red as he summoned the courage to address her, afraid of sounding foolish. "This book is about *fictional* trolls," he blurted finally. "I want a book about real trolls, woodland trolls preferably."

The librarian approached and peered down at Jules once more through the shiny lenses of her oversized glasses. "You're that Jules boy, aren't you?" she said, snatching the book away from him. "I've heard the others talking about you. I haven't seen you here before, maybe we should keep it that way." And with that she was gone, gone with the fictional troll book, and somehow Jules had the sinking feeling she wasn't going to return with a book about real woodland trolls.

Jules ran out as fast as he could.

With nowhere else to go, he retraced his steps and headed toward home. As he dawdled down the long road, however, he decided that he didn't feel like going back to the store quite yet. His mother would just find some other mindless chore for him to do, like scrubbing the walls or smashing all the spider webs with the broom (which always made him feel guilty). This was a rare free day; he might as well enjoy it to the fullest. So when he was about a half-mile from The Beanery, he abruptly changed direction and turned down an old dirt path, long overgrown with brambles and blanketed with mildewed leaves, which led into the forest.

The area surrounding Jules's home consisted mostly of unexplored woodlands. He had never ventured too far into the forest, always afraid of what lived there. His father had told him stories of wild boars and wolves that hunted children for sport, and of old women who would bewitch you and make you do all sorts of horrible things if you weren't careful. There were other people who lived there, too. These were mostly the harmless kind that weren't quite right in the head, but there were also tales about dangerous people, criminals or outlaws mostly, who resided in the forest among the tallest trees, emerging every now and then to cause mischief. Added to the danger was the fact that the outer fringe of the woods was crisscrossed with dozens of intersecting paths and it was easy to lose your way if you weren't careful. Deep inside the forest there were no trails and nobody seemed to know what was to be found there.

On this day, though, Jules just wanted to get away, and he marched down the dirt path until it ended abruptly. The forest here was crowded with elms and pines, and a thick layer of leaves and needles blanketed the ground. He began to feel more cheerful, for it was very cool and peaceful, when he stumbled across a small clearing.

He sat down in the soft moss with his back against a tree. *Well,* he thought, *it certainly is pleasant enough. Perhaps all of those old stories are only meant to scare kids, and there really isn't anything dangerous here at all.* He heard a rustle on the forest floor. Startled, Jules turned suddenly, and then laughed out loud when he discovered it was merely a pair of squirrels scavenging for acorns.

Jules watched the two animals forage for a few minutes, then shut his eyes while he listened to the various sounds of the forest. There was an odd rhythm to it all. It was as if he were the conductor of a wonderful orchestra, and that the bird calls, creaking branches, and crunching of the leaves were part of a thrilling symphony. He heard another crunch off to the left, louder than before, but this time he didn't turn.

Moments later Jules felt a blast of hot breath on his neck. Startled, he opened his eyes just as he heard a low-pitched growl from behind the tree. He didn't wait to find out what it was. He jumped up and bolted out of the clearing, without looking back. He thought he heard something charging after him, but Jules was small and could dart here and there between the tree trunks, and he was able to squeeze through the thickets where he couldn't be followed. The footsteps grew faint. Whatever the thing was—a wild animal, someone playing a trick on him, or just a figment of his imagination—was gone. He was safe.

Jules paused to catch his breath, and to give his heart a chance to stop pounding. It was then that he realized that, even if he had escaped from whatever had been chasing him, he had lost the path, and with it, his way. He thought again of some of the stories his father had told him about witches and ogres that lived deep in the woods and shivered, wondering if he'd ever find his way home again. Without knowing what else to do, he began wandering through the forest, hoping to retrace his steps and accidentally stumble across one of the winding dirt paths. Unknowingly, he turned completely in the wrong direction and moved deeper and deeper into the woods.

He had been walking for nearly half an hour when he found a wide clearing of thick grass nestled inside a ring of silver-barked beeches. And he was no longer alone, for not twenty feet away was the very same troll he had encountered the previous night. It was still wearing the burlap fragment for a shirt, but now there were a few twigs and leaves in its hair. The troll was busy picking purple and red berries from a nearby bush and wasn't paying the slightest attention to Jules whatsoever.

Jules considered what to do next. He didn't know whether it would be safe to go up to this creature, for while it certainly had seemed harmless enough during their first encounter, Jules was clearly in its natural environment and it might not appreciate having its lunch interrupted. He was now painfully aware that there were dangerous things in this forest, and this troll could be one of them. Eventually, though, Jules recalled that this little troll had been thoughtful enough to sort the entire vat of coffee beans after he had fallen asleep, and concluded the troll was probably unlikely to be dangerous, or it would have harmed him when it had the chance. Besides, if he asked politely, it might help him find his way home, and that was certainly worth the risk. He walked toward the troll, slowly, so as to not startle it.

"Excuse me," Jules said in his most pleasant voice. "I don't suppose you could tell me how to get back to my house?"

The troll continued picking berries, one after another, and didn't respond.

Jules began to wonder if his mind was playing tricks on him. "I say, excuse me," he said, a bit louder this time.

"About time you got here," the troll said without even bothering to turn its head. "I've been listening to you tromp through the forest for the past ten minutes. An elephant couldn't make more noise."

"I was starting to think you weren't actually here," Jules said. "Are you real?"

"I'm as real as you are, boy," said the troll. "Bergen the Woodland Troll, at yer service."

"Jules the . . . well, I'm just a boy. We say 'glad to meet you' but I think it means the same thing."

"Well, then, glad t' meetcha, Jules the well-I'm-just-a-boy."

"The same to you."

Then Jules remembered his manners, and said, "Oh, by the way, thanks for sorting those beans for me last night. It was worth it just to see my mother's face."

"Don't you often see her face?"

"Not when it looks like that. It had a funny expression on it. Sort of like when you think you are about to drink a glass of orange juice and it turns out to be milk instead."

"Happy to be of assistance," Bergen answered. "It didn't take very long, and I took a few extra-juicy specimens for myself. I figured you wouldn't mind."

"I don't mind. I wish I'd thought to bring some more for you, but I didn't know I'd be seeing you again."

"Thanks anyway. It's the thought that counts."

Jules wasn't quite sure what to say next, and so used the opportunity to look at the little creature more closely, quite forgetting that it was considered impolite to stare. The troll stared back at him like it was the natural thing to do, reaching down from time to time to scratch his stomach. After a minute of this, the troll blinked twice, shrugged his shoulders, and then stretched up his arms to continue tugging on the bush in an attempt to reach a few juicy, ripe berries that were just beyond his reach.

"Here, let me." Jules reached up and picked a few dozen berries from the upper branches and set them on the ground by Bergen's feet. To a creature his size, the tiny berries were as big as full-grown oranges or grapefruit, and it took several bites for

Bergen to chew through each of them. Eventually, the odd little creature remembered his manners and offered a wrinkly berry to Jules, who politely declined the offer.

"What I don't understand," Jules said, changing the subject, "is why you were sneaking around in the middle of the night and trying to steal some of our coffee beans in the first place."

Bergen wagged his head emphatically. "No, not steal—at least not in the *first place*, as you put it. I was always quite willing to pay for those beans."

"Then why didn't you just come through the front door?"

"I've learned it's best to stay out of sight. Sometimes you humans react poorly to us trolls." To make his point, Bergen made a face as if he saw something frightful off in the distance and pretended to faint. Then he popped up off the ground, laughed hysterically, and shrugged. "Oh, well. Can't be responsible fer what others think of you. Let that be a lesson to you, boy."

Jules thought that over and wondered whether this troll had been what had scared him earlier, maybe as a joke. He decided not to bring it up. "I'll bet my father wouldn't have thought about it twice. A sale is a sale, he always said. Besides, he was always telling stories about ogres and fairies and other such creatures. He wouldn't have been afraid of you."

"Your father? Your father was the worst of all, but not because he was afraid. More than once me an' my friends came to his store an' tried to buy a bagful of those delicious roasted beans, but each time he told us that our money wasn't good there, an' chased us away. He just didn't care for my species, is all. Prejudiced, he was. Thought beans were just fer humans."

"Maybe you didn't have the right kind of money."

"You think we tried to pay with rocks or sticks?"

Bergen fished something out from his pocket and flipped it through the air. Jules caught it in his palm and looked it over. It was a small coin, unlike any he'd ever seen before, and surprisingly heavy. One thing was certain: it was gold. Jules was sure of that. Why had his father turned the trolls down? They could have been rich!

"He wouldn't take it, and told us not to come back," Bergen said. "Not me, not any of my friends. Since then, I've stayed away, mostly. But last night I was so hungry, and the smell of fresh beans was just so . . . so . . . so . . ." Bergen shut his eyes and inhaled deeply through his nose. "Temptation and all that, ya know." He burped.

"It doesn't matter anymore," Jules said. "My father's dead now."

"I know."

"But if you can show me the way home," Jules said, "I'll let you return to the store anytime for as many beans as you want."

"Do you really mean it? That's awful kind of you, boy."

"Just make sure it's at night, after my mother has gone to bed, okay? There's no telling how she'd react if she saw you."

"Thanks, boy. I might just do that. Glad t'meetcha an' all that." Bergen turned and headed back toward the thicket.

"Wait!" Jules cried. "Don't leave yet! You didn't answer my question. Where am I? I mean, how do I get home?"

"You were serious." Bergen shook his head.

"Yes; I'm lost. If you don't help me, I'll never find my way back. Please, can't you help me?"

Bergen sighed, and then extended a gnarly index finger. Once again, the troll turned to run off.

"Wait!" Jules cried again. "Your coin! Here, take it back."

But the troll would have none of it. "Keep it, boy," he said. "For yer troubles—and yer beans." The little creature scooted across the clearing, but before disappearing into the underbrush he stopped and turned to face Jules once more. "I almost forgot why I was lookin' for you. There's goin' to be a meetin' on Friday night. Consider yerself invited."

"A meeting? What about?"

"You'll see."

"Who'll be there? Other trolls?"

"So many questions! Just be at the conference room at midnight. Don't be late. And fer goodness sakes, try not to break anythin.'"

"The conference room? Where's that? I don't understand."

Bergen sighed. "Sure, boy, you've been there before. I've seen ya throwin' pebbles at the windows."

"Throwing pebbles? What—oh, you mean the Klepner house. I thought that place was haunted."

"Not haunted, but maybe there are things worse than ghosts."

Jules was still considering the meaning of those words when he realized the little fellow was gone. Once again he was all alone, but now he was no longer worried about finding his way home. With a cheerful bounce in his step, he started off in the direction that Bergen had pointed. Sure enough, not more than forty-five minutes later, he reached the edge of the forest, and somehow even stumbled upon the correct path. He was home by dinnertime, with a half an hour to spare.

CHAPTER 4

The Secret Meeting

The next few days seemed to drag on forever until Friday evening finally arrived. When it was close to midnight, Jules opened his door and listened until he heard the rhythmic snoring coming from his mother's bedroom. He tiptoed down the hall with his heart pounding and his breath resonating in his ears. To this point, it had all seemed like a dream: catching a troll—*a troll of all things!*—trying to make off with a sack of coffee beans; conversing with it while lost in the forest; being invited to a mysterious meeting. Until now he didn't take it all very seriously; the encounters with the strange little creature seemed to happen to some other boy while he stood by and watched from a distance. Now, though, he had to admit that all of it *was* real and it *was* happening to him. Moreover, he had an odd feeling he was about to begin some horrible adventure that, once started, couldn't be stopped. And it would all start here, by sneaking off into the night while his mother slept in the next room. Yet to his everlasting credit Jules didn't hesitate. Entering the darkened store, he quietly unlatched the front lock, slipped through the doorway, and bounded down the walk.

It was a clear and humid June night. The moon shone like a beacon, but the light was unnecessary, for Jules knew the way—very well, in fact. He remembered where to high-step over each gnarly root and when to duck to avoid a painful slap in the face from the prickly branches that hung low over the path. Jules was following an old dirt trail that hugged the edge of the forest. This was the quickest way, for, like his home, the Klepner house backed up against the woods. There was also a paved road for cars, but it took the long way around and he wanted to avoid being seen by one of his neighbors, who he feared would report the incident to his mother, and then there would be all hell to pay. No, he would take the path and stay out of sight. He never considered that at night the woods harbored much more dangerous and frightening things than he could possibly encounter along the road.

But on this particular night nothing terrible happened, and after roughly half an hour, Jules reached the rotting Klepner house. He looked up at the decrepit structure and trembled. In the bright moonlight it glowed with a pale, ominous sheen, reminding Jules of haunted mansions in horror stories his father used to tell him. Strange, disjointed details caught his attention: the paint flaking from the shutters; the overgrown garden; the weeds sprouting through the stones in the walk. One window pane on the second story was shattered, evidence of his one successful pebble toss during the previous fall. A few shards of glass glistened below it, near the flower bed.

"Well, here goes," Jules muttered. He took a deep breath as he tried to steady his nerves. "How scary can they be anyway? They're not even a foot tall. Probably just want to climb into my pockets or something." With that thought, he reached into his coat pocket and felt around with his stubby fingers. Yes, the hazelnut-flavored coffee beans were still there. At the last moment he had thrown on the jacket and grabbed a handful of coffee beans and shoved them into the pocket. It was always good to have a peace offering handy in case one was needed, he had decided, even if the price was wearing a jacket on a hot night.

Gathering all his inner strength, he walked up to the front door, turned the knob, and pushed. The door was unlocked and swung open with a faint squeak. He held his breath and walked in.

It took a moment for his eyes to get accustomed to the darkness—for it *was* dark, much darker than out on the porch underneath the nearly full moon and an umbrella of glittering stars. The room was completely empty, which struck him as quite peculiar. Somehow the absence of furniture made the house seem lifeless, and it reminded him of an overcast winter afternoon when everything is cold and gray outside.

The paint was peeling from the walls in spots, although not as badly as outside the house, and a thin blanket of dust covered the floor. In places he could make out tiny mouse prints, but there was no evidence that anything bigger had been here. Either this so-called meeting was a hoax, or there was another way in. He quietly shut the door behind him.

Well, he thought, *what do I do now?* He ran his hand along the back of his neck. The tiny hairs were standing on end as if they were electrified. He was struck by a sudden wave of self-doubt. Maybe he should turn around and go home before anything happened to him. He reached out for the doorknob. But then Jules felt a yearning grow from deep inside him, a desire to shed his old skin and become someone other than the quiet, insecure boy who was the source of all the schoolyard jokes. For the first time in his life, he felt the call of adventure. Maybe it was nothing more than the remnants of stories his father had read to him that were still rattling around inside his head, a dim memory of heroes on impossible quests with nothing but their courage and wits to guide them, but for whatever reason, he dropped his hand back to his side.

"No," he said. "I've come this far. Perhaps no one is here, but I'll never know if I don't look around a bit."

Walking past the coat closet and deeper into the house, Jules passed through the empty living room and soon found what was quite obviously the kitchen. It was darker in this part of the house, for there were fewer windows. Through the gloom he noticed that the stove and refrigerator were missing. A row of wood cabinets protruded from the wall. In the middle of the room a chandelier hung from the ceiling, cobwebs spun between its brass arms. Jules felt along the wall and flicked the light switch. No luck; the room remained dark.

Maybe there was something interesting in one of the cabinets. He swung open the nearest door and anxiously reached his hand inside and felt around: empty. He tried the others, and inside the very last cabinet his hand grasped something hard. He jumped, startled, before realizing that it was nothing but half of a thick wax candle. Next to it was a matchbook. With a joyful shout, Jules struck a match and lit the wick. A soft glow filled the room, and Jules could see better almost immediately. He slipped the remaining matches into one of his pockets and, after confirming that the other cabinets were indeed empty, he continued through the house, eventually locating a flight of stairs leading up.

On the second floor he discovered three bedrooms and a bathroom. Unlike the living room downstairs, these still contained furniture—dressers and desks mostly, with the occasional nightstand and floor lamp. A bedroom window was shattered, and a small stone lay on the floor. Jules picked it up; it fit perfectly into his palm. There was no doubt this was his handiwork. With a guilty pang in his stomach, he placed the stone neatly on the desk, but then thought better of it and slipped it into his pocket next to the matches.

Overcome with curiosity, Jules rifled through all the drawers, finding them empty except for some yellowed pieces of paper scattered inside a desk. In one of the closets, though, he discovered a dusty old-fashioned hat, a gray fedora just like the one his father was wearing in the picture that sat on the mantle above the fireplace in the living room. It was the only image of his father in his entire house, a little framed portrait that his mother had purchased on their third anniversary, before Jules was even born. Other than that photo, this hat was the only fedora he had ever seen. He brushed away some of the dust and cobwebs and placed the ragged hat on his head. It slipped down to the bridge of his nose, and the dust made him sneeze twice.

Discouraged, he took it off. He thought he would look quite nice in such a hat and that at the very least it would make a good souvenir. At that moment, though, he noticed a narrow leather flap lining the inside rim, and he had an idea. He went back and collected several of the yellowed papers from the desk, folded them into strips, and slipped them behind the flap. Sure enough, the hat now fit. Proud of his ingenuity, he marched into the bathroom and stood in front of the mirror.

The hat was wrinkled and stained and made his ears stick out.

Jules loved it.

He swung the mirror open, and in the medicine cabinet he discovered a partially-used stick of cherry-red lipstick. Jules removed the cap and touched it. After years of nonuse, the lipstick had crusted over and hardened.

"It feels like a crayon," Jules muttered. He knew what to do with crayons. Giggling with delight, he drew large swoops across the mirror. Then suddenly embarrassed at his childishness, he stopped what he was doing, absentmindedly pocketed the lipstick, and headed back downstairs.

Well, he thought to himself. *I've now explored the entire house and haven't found anything out of the ordinary. It looks as if there was no meeting after all. Probably just my imagination from the start.* Yet he was not in the least disappointed, for he was proud of his daring escapade, proud that he saw it through to the end and didn't turn back earlier when he had the chance.

Thinking this was to be the end of his midnight adventure, Jules headed toward the front door, still grasping the lit candle in his right hand.

It was then that he noticed a light flickering from underneath the coat closet door!

Slowly, he turned the knob and tugged the door open. Why, it wasn't a closet after all! Rickety wooden stairs led down into the darkness—to a basement, perhaps—and by listening carefully, he could just make out the low hum of conversation. Without considering the possible consequences, he began to make his way down. At the third step there was a loud creak, and instantly the murmuring stopped.

Well, now I've done it, Jules thought. There was no turning back; whatever was in the basement now knew he was there. With a sigh, he resumed his descent.

When he had nearly reached the bottom of the stairs, a gruff voice called out, "Who goes there? Begone!"

Screwing up all his courage, Jules stammered, "I—my name is Jules. A troll—I mean Bergen—he's a woodland troll—he asked me to come."

The murmuring picked up again, louder than before, and because he wasn't told anything to the contrary, Jules walked down the remaining few stairs.

He found himself in a large room, lit dimly by a collection of colorful thick candles scattered around the floor. Jules jumped in surprise, and a little bit of fear, too. For instead of a few tiny woodland trolls, the room was filled with the most remarkable collection of extraordinary-looking creatures. None were human; that much was obvious. It wasn't that they had the wrong number of arms or eyes or anything like that, just that their shape and proportions were off. Most were sitting on metal folding chairs arranged around a long rectangular table.

What have I gotten myself into now? Jules asked himself. He stared wide-eyed, trying to peer through the shadows. He caught glimpses of forms moving in the darkness. On one side of the table, he saw a furry lemur-like creature sipping from a large mug, dribbling drops of yellowish liquid from its chin. Across from him, another creature with long, muscular arms and skin that looked like tree bark whispered to a short, stout thing with a long frizzy beard. Next to them, a waif-like being with stringy white hair watched Jules with deep green eyes. At the close end of the table, something with brown leathery skin and a head shaped like a watermelon impatiently drummed its long, thick fingers on the tabletop. In all, there were more than a dozen different types of creatures huddled around the table. Jules inhaled sharply and nearly coughed, for the place stank like rotting eggs and farm animals.

As his eyes continued to adjust, his gaze fixed on the head of the room (that is, the point farthest from the foot of the stairs), where sat the largest creature Jules had ever seen up close. It was sitting directly on the floor, with both its elbows propped on the table and its knees pulled to its chest. Its head was enormous, nearly as broad as its chest (which itself was as wide as a barrel), and it stared at Jules with eyes as black as the night. As Jules took all this in, he realized that the creature bore an odd resemblance to the gigantic troll whose picture graced the cover of that dopey library book, *Trolls: Their Habits and History*, which he had dismissed so quickly as fiction. He wondered if the library lady would let him check it out if he returned.

"WHO ARE YOU?" this monstrous creature demanded in the deep, rumbling voice Jules had heard moments earlier.

"He's wi' me," said a familiar high-pitched squeal from the corner.

Jules turned. Sure enough, sitting in a rickety chair far too big for him was that peculiar woodland troll who had egged him into coming here. Even though there were several empty seats around the table, Bergen must not have been considered important enough to be permitted to sit alongside the others.

"EXPLAIN YOURSELF!" the huge creature thundered.

After an uncomfortable silence, Bergen stammered, "Well, er, I invited 'im."

Before the gigantic creature had had the opportunity to chastise him a second time, the little troll launched into a synopsis of their initial meeting, emphasizing how Jules had captured him with nothing but his bare hands, using only his quick wits and fast reflexes.

It didn't quite happen like that, thought Jules as he listened to Bergen's account. For one thing, the tiny troll neglected to mention that Jules was scared half to death, and that he'd used the old wooden bucket for the actual capturing. For another, the little fellow conveniently left out the purpose of his visit to the store that night, and that he was caught red-handed trying to sneak away with a sack filled with coffee beans. Jules didn't dare interrupt, though. He was secretly thrilled at being called *quick-witted*—how he wished the other kids at school could hear that description—and he gathered that getting caught was bad enough, but getting caught under a bucket by a frightened boy—well, that would be unforgivable!

"And then he just released me un'armed," concluded Bergen with a flourish, regaining some of his confidence.

"So for this you invited him to our secret meeting," the huge monster growled. "The boy let you go, no doubt because you were too small and bony for him to roast for dinner, and as a result you told him about this private conference."

"No, no; not just," Bergen replied.

"I wasn't going to *eat* him," Jules whispered softly.

"I'll never understand your kind," the large troll scolded, wagging his head slowly from side to side. "Very well, you invited him. There's no need for him to stay. Dis-invite him."

"I believe," said another voice from across the room, "that the correct word is 'uninvite.'"

"Disinvite, uninvite," the large troll replied wearily. "I don't see the difference. Just pick one or the other and get it over with."

"I won't do the one, or the other," Bergen retorted. "He's my friend, and besides—"

"He is just a boy, a toddler," scoffed a raspy voice. "Can't have him involved with this sort of trouble."

"Go home, lad," another creature said from close to where Jules stood. "Go back to your mama's store, and grow old and gray, and forget about this night! For you will live a far more comfortable life without being encumbered by the knowledge of our dark business."

"Indubitably!"

"Yes, yes!"

"Go home!"

"I think that's the kid I scared in the forest."

"He's not wanted!"

"Pass the ale."

"ENOUGH!" the humungous troll bellowed, frowning from beneath its bushy eyebrows. Instantly the bickering among the other creatures ended and the basement became so quiet that Jules could hear his heart thumping inside his chest. If there had been any remaining doubt that the enormous creature at the end of the table was in charge of the proceedings, that one word (and the resulting reaction) had eliminated it.

Jules heard himself speak up, louder than before, still basking in the thrill of being called quick-witted. "If I may, sir, I'd like to stay, even for just a little while." His courage surprised him, but it seemed as if these creatures weren't going to hurt him after all. In fact, they seemed more concerned for him than dangerous—at least those that had spoken up, that is.

The huge creature sighed, lifted its eyebrows, and stared hard into Jules's eyes. To Jules, its face was worn with memories both terrible and marvelous, but he couldn't help but think it looked tired. "Very well," it said at last. "This business involves you too, in a way. Go take a seat in the corner."

Jules saw Bergen jumping up and down on his seat, waving with excitement and pointing to the empty chair next to him.

"I guess I'll try over there," Jules said with a smile.

"I thought you'd never come," Bergen whispered, once Jules had blown out his candle and sat down. "Missed the preliminaries."

"I'm sorry," Jules said. "I—"

"*Shhhhhhh!*" hissed another creature seated at the table, hidden in the darkness.

"Nice hat," Bergen whispered after a long pause.

Jules smiled. Then, remembering the gift he had brought, he reached into his pocket and pulled out a half-dozen coffee beans and passed them to the little troll. Bergen smiled in gratitude and popped one in his mouth, putting the remainder on the edge of his chair for a later snack.

"Very well," the large troll said in its now-familiar deep rumbling voice. "I expect that we will have no more interruptions." It stared long and hard at Jules, its huge eyes glistening underneath the thick eyebrows.

"That's Thisted," Bergen whispered between bites. "He's a mountain troll. Probably best to stay on his good side."

Jules gulped, nodded his head quickly, and looked down at his sneakers until he no longer felt the heat from the creature's piercing gaze.

After a long pause, Thisted spoke once more. "There is nothing more for us to do," he said. "And so this will likely be our last council meeting. We have failed in our endeavor."

This announcement seemed to cause some dismay among the other creatures gathered in the basement, and order broke down once more in a cacophony of shouts and side conversations. In the middle of it all, Jules thought he heard the words "Eldritch girl" and the phrase "would have done just fine." The large troll seemed to ignore this outburst, or perhaps didn't hear it at all.

Then Bergen climbed up on the table. "Why not try this boy?" he asked, quite evidently meaning Jules. "As I was trying to say earlier before bein' interrupted, I didn't only invite him to this meetin' because he released me. He may be the One we've been searchin' for."

"No, it cannot be," Thisted said, slowly wagging his head from side to side. "You do not understand, for you are young and this has been your first council-cycle. There are dangerous things about this boy, things you do not know about. He could be the downfall of us all."

Now what could that mean, Jules wondered. During his short life he had been described many ways, but 'dangerous' was never one of them, at least until now. Why, he was the least dangerous person he knew, unless you counted the times he hurt himself by accident, such as when he stabbed his leg with a pencil while skipping down the school hall. There was still a piece of graphite lodged under his skin, a small black smudge that looked like a dark freckle. But there was a sharpness to the troll's tone that suggested that he was referring to something entirely different. As Jules tried to make sense of it, the room was once again filled with wild shouts.

"Dangerous!"

"Would destroy everything."

"No harm in letting him try."

"Preposterous!"

"More ale, over here!"

"We are running out of time," implored a short, squat creature. "We must act forthwith!"

"Forthwith and fifthwith, I'd say," another creature answered.

"Sixthwith!" another cried, raising the ante.

"This is getting us nowhere," Thisted interrupted.

"Consider the consequences," said Bergen, who was still standing firmly on the tabletop, despite the frantic attempts by some of the other creatures to shoo him off with their hands. "Are you afraid that he'll fail?"

"No," the huge mountain troll replied. "I am afraid that he'll succeed, but not in the way we expect."

"I hardly believe," Bergen countered, once the next round of catcalls and murmurings had quieted down enough for him to continue, "that it would be better to do nothin' than to take the chance this boy will be able to save things. You're sentencin' our world to death."

"Then there's no point saving the rest of that there ale for next time, is there?" a roundish creature called out, followed by a pronounced burp. "Send it back this way, would you? Now there's a good fellow."

"Seize the day!" a voice shouted from the side of the room to a chorus of cheers, as the jug was passed along the table.

"Fortune favors the bold!"

"No sooner said than done!"

"E pluribus unum!"

"Beware of the dog!"

"I don't mean to interrupt," Jules interrupted, "but it seems as though I may be of assistance in some way. I'm not very good at solving problems, but if you explain what you need help with, perhaps I can come up with some suggestions. I guess what I'm trying to say is: maybe I could hear the whole story from the beginning?"

"Oh very well," Thisted said in his low, rumbling voice. "Although I hardly see the point of it. This council has been convened to address a terrifying circumstance."

"Alarming!"

"Shocking!"

"Distressing!"

"Quiet," Thisted warned. "Or I'll never get through it before morning." He glared around the room until order was restored.

He continued, "You see, our world is dying."

The mountain troll stopped then and peered at Jules from underneath his bushy eyebrows. Jules suddenly realized that all the creatures were staring at him. Feeling strangely self-conscious, Jules blushed and nodded his understanding, and waited for the large creature to continue his narration.

"Our crops are withering; our trees are dying. But that's not all. Everything is being *worn away*. The landscape is melting into nothingness, like ice cream left out in the sun."

"That sounds horrible!" Jules exclaimed. "But what is causing it? Is it some parasite? Our yard was once infested with mole crickets and grubs and had to be sprayed. I couldn't walk on it for two weeks."

Thisted glanced at the other creatures gathered around the basement. "We do not know the cause of this trouble," he continued. "But as for what can be done, that is the purpose of this council, as you have no doubt gathered. If we do not find a solution, our entire world will soon become uninhabitable, and everything in it will perish."

As he paused to collect his thoughts, a pale green creature that looked surprisingly like an uncooked stalk of broccoli stood and waved for some quiet. "The little troll makes sense for once," it said over the persistent sound of clinking glass. "Why *not* use this child? We must act now, or all will be permanently lost. All your fears may turn out to be unfounded." It spoke so fast and soft that Jules could hardly make out the next words from his seat near the corner. "At any rate, the boy appears human, and at this point we must be willing to take risks."

"Looks can be deceiving," a voice shouted from the darkness.

"A pig wearing lipstick is still a pig."

"Don't judge a book by its cover."

"A rose is a rose is a rose."

"I think I'd like to help you, if there's some way that I can," Jules said quietly. After another uncomfortable silence, he asked, "Where is this land of yours, anyway? I'm very curious about new places, you know."

Thisted sat still for a few moments with his eyes shut and his hands folded across his knees. Then the massive troll opened his eyes, looked into Jules's face, sighed heavily, banged a knee against the edge of the table, cursed softly, and seemed to reach a decision. "Go on, Hortlax," Thisted prodded. "You might as well show it to him."

Hortlax—that is, the broccoli stalk—reached down and pulled a large but thin book from a worn satchel that had been hidden under the table. Hortlax held the book carefully in his hands, and Jules quickly understood why, for it looked like it would crumble to dust if someone so much as breathed on it the wrong way. The book was bound by a weathered and cracked brown leather cover that was spotted with black stains. On the front was a picture of a white bird with outstretched wings. Encircling the bird were three snakes that were biting each other's tails, forming an unbroken ring. From where Jules sat, there didn't appear to be any words or letters of any kind.

Hortlax plopped the book in the middle of the table, raising a small cloud of dust, and swung the book open to a page marked by a ribbon bookmark.

"Ooh, it's a map," Jules remarked from the corner. He adored maps, always had since he was a little boy. He still remembered how his father would hold him in his arms so he could study the yellowed map of Scandinavia that hung on the living room wall, and how his father would point out the rivers, the mountains, the fjords, the roads. How his father would laugh good-naturedly as Jules would struggle to pronounce some of the odd-sounding towns and villages marked in red and black ink. Then his father would talk about some of the people who lived there, about their daily lives and their grand adventures. When Jules would ask how he knew all this, his father would just laugh and wink, but never answered the question.

Jules really missed those times. That old map still decorated the wall and he still pored over all its details, but now, without his father around, Jules could only wonder what was happening in all those towns and villages and to the people that Jules once regarded as friends. At any rate, Jules had become quite adept at understanding maps, which had once been confusing and complicated to him.

But as Jules watched from his seat, large dark blobs formed unevenly inside the book and bubbled together until the map faded away into nothingness, leaving just blank pages behind. "What happened?" he asked, disappointed. "Where did it go?"

Thisted stared at Jules again with his unflinching gaze, and for a moment Jules thought he was going to be chastised once more for speaking out of turn. Instead, though, Thisted made a subtle movement with his hand, and Jules realized with surprise that he was being motioned to come closer.

As Jules approached, he glanced once more at the large book, still sprawled across the table. Now here was a shock—the pages were no longer blank. But instead of a map, a whirlwind of colors swirled across the pages, almost as if they weren't sure where they belonged, or possibly as if they knew but were just taking their time getting there. Eventually, though, the colors finally seemed to sort themselves out and a picture began to form. No—not just a picture. It was the map again, but somehow it didn't look quite the same as the one he had peered at from across the room, although he wasn't sure why. Maybe it was because the angle was different.

Then Jules gasped, for, unlike any map that he had ever seen before, this one was *three-dimensional*. Whereas most maps are flat and rely on colors and symbols to represent features like roads and rivers and libraries and mountains and things like that, this one rose up—no, make that *jumped* up—from the page. Why hadn't he noticed that from his seat in the corner? He stared hard at the expanding features. He saw a long chain of mountains stretching from the north to the southwest. On one side of the mountain range there extended a beige and featureless plain, and Jules instantly recognized this to be an immense inhospitable desert. Past the desert was a swath of blue which he took to be a great inland sea. Most of the map, though, was green, quite clearly a forest. The map contained little true detail, as if Jules was viewing it through foggy glasses.

Enraptured, Jules stared and stared, and soon discovered that particular sections seemed to expand when his eyes focused on them, as if he was looking through a great magnifying glass, while other areas simultaneously darkened and shrunk away into the background. As he learned to use this ability, he focused on particular areas of the map and gradually discerned more and more detail. He spied rivers and grasslands, hilltops and valleys. He saw a ring of clouds circling the mountaintops, above which poked some of the very highest snow-capped peaks. He noticed a great canyon shaped like a half moon. Mist rose from a series of eight thunderous waterfalls cascading along a turbulent river. An archipelago of two dozen islands was scattered across the vast sea. And there were lakes, too, hundreds and thousands of ice-blue lakes that marred the otherwise green landscape.

Jules could have been looking at the map for a minute, or ten minutes, he really didn't know, nor did he care. Soon he was able to locate towns and villages scattered here and there, some connected by a network of roads, but who—or what—lived in them he could not tell.

Thisted sighed. "This is our world, boy."

"It's very pretty," Jules said, perking up. By now he had gotten over his initial fear of these creatures, and he spoke up without hesitation. "Can I go there? How far away is it?"

At that Hortlax pointed at one of the corners of the map. By leaning close and squinting his eyes the right amount, Jules could identify a small house. It glowed red.

"The map reveals itself," Hortlax said softly. "That is where we are, now."

Then Jules focused his eyes as hard as he could and noticed a tiny road leading a very short distance along the rim of the map, along the outer edge of the forest. He traced it with his finger, so as not to lose the thread of it, until he came to another tiny house. This house was blue and had a porch in the back.

His house.

"Are you telling me that this is a map of the woods behind my home?" Jules asked, feeling a bit foolish. A walnut-sized lump rose in the back of his throat. None of this made any sense. It couldn't be real; none of this could be real. "That can't be right! I see snow-capped mountains. And look at that river! It must be at least a half mile wide. Those measly woods outside aren't nearly big enough for all of that. Why, it is only an hour to—." Here he named a nearby town, just on the other side of the forest. "I went there once on a field trip. We went to an aquarium and I touched a sting ray. It was soft and velvety. We certainly didn't pass by any mountains or deserts; I'd remember that, I think."

"All is as the map reveals," Thisted growled cryptically.

"You see, Jules," said a short, pudgy creature with a cantaloupe-shaped head. "Our world touches yours on its edges, but it's bigger on the inside than on the outside, if you catch my meaning."

Jules did *not* grasp its meaning one bit, but it didn't really bother him at the moment, for he couldn't resist examining the map further. He was fascinated by it, drawn to it by some unexplainable urge, and found he couldn't look away. The detail was marvelous. He now noticed great flocks of birds crossing over the enormous forests, and vast herds of large animals covering some of the golden plains. He stared at the great river, and thought he saw long flatboats floating on it. He glanced once more at the image of his house in the corner and spied some movement in the woods nearby. It looked like a pair of horses, but what would anyone be doing out on a horse in the forest in the middle of the night?

Before he could look any closer, though, Thisted nodded briefly to Hortlax, who grasped the cover of the book and swung it shut with a loud thump. The map faded away into nothingness, and Jules wondered whether he would ever have an opportunity to study it again. Hortlax lifted the book from the table and slipped it back into the worn satchel, out of sight.

Jules silently considered what he had just seen. *Our crops are withering; our trees are dying,* Thisted had said. Was that really true? He wondered. It certainly didn't appear that there was anything wrong with their world. Either the map was wrong, or Thisted was lying about something. He began to ask a question, then changed his mind and shut his mouth before any words came forth. For some reason he thought it better not to say anything. Besides, Bergen had already warned that it was best to stay on the mountain troll's good side, and he didn't want to appear impolite.

Suddenly Jules felt very sleepy. Whether it was the late hour or the initial excitement of his adventure wearing off, or possibly the strain of focusing so intently on the map for such a long period of time, he found he could hardly keep his eyes open. And so, as the odd creatures continued their discussion and ale-drinking, his consciousness gradually faded away to nothingness.

CHAPTER 5

Store Help

Jules awoke with his head pounding and his clothes drenched in sweat. He had forgotten to change into his pajamas again. Groaning, he scrambled off his sleeping bag, opened the door, and stepped straight into the harsh sunbeam streaming through the windows.

I must have overslept, he realized.

The house was quiet. His mother must have gone into town, perhaps to buy some supplies. Jules considered it odd that she would run off without waking him first—who would watch the store?—but thought no more about it. He got dressed and devoured a grapefruit and two pieces of white toast for breakfast (a little burned, just the way he liked it), washed down by a glass of orange juice mixed with a spoonful of sugar.

As he ate, the events of the previous evening flooded back. He remembered sneaking into the Klepner house in the middle of the night, stumbling into the basement, and witnessing a bizarre meeting with strange-looking creatures. Bergen was one of them, he decided. There was a map, too. Yes, of course. He concentrated hard and tried to visualize the map inside his head. It was odd, but before now, he couldn't recall ever *wanting* to remember something that he saw in a book. Maybe it was because he had such trouble reading words the right way.

Maybe that's what had caused his headache.

But how had he gotten home? Now that he thought about it, Jules couldn't remember returning to the store after the meeting was over. Perhaps he had fallen asleep in the Klepner basement, and the strange creatures had brought him here. He giggled at the mental image of the gigantic mountain troll Thisted walking along the road, carrying him over his enormous head like a ragdoll and depositing him on his bed before disappearing into the night. Of course, that wasn't possible. For one thing, that enormous creature would never have fit through the doorway.

Maybe it was all a dream, or his imagination.

He reached into his pocket and was surprised to find the coin that Bergen had given him in the forest several days earlier. That answered that. He wondered if it was worth anything. Was it really made out of gold, or was it some fake? He decided it was something to investigate. Perhaps The Beanery was about to get some new customers. According to Bergen, Jules's father wasn't interested in selling beans to him or his impish woodland troll friends, but maybe that had been a bad decision. It was time to find out. He scribbled a note for his mother, tacked it to the kitchen door, and skipped down the walk toward town.

He knew where he was going, a coin shop on the corner of Fourth and Main. Jules had never been inside, but he had noticed the shiny window displays in the past. After some time, he reached the store and pushed open the heavy glass door. He heard a bell tinkle brightly.

The store was dark, damp. The carpet was stained in places and smelled funny. An old golden retriever sat near the door, and as Jules walked by, it raised its head and wagged its tail with a minimal amount of energy.

Behind the counter stood an elderly man who was carefully studying a coin through a tiny loupe plastered against his right eye.

"Excuse me," Jules said. He had walked all the way up to the counter and waited patiently for two full minutes for the man to look up from his work.

The man put down the loupe and peered over the top of his glasses. "Yes? Can I help you?"

Jules stood on his toes so the man could now see his entire head over the edge of the counter. "Can you tell me what a coin is worth?"

The man looked curiously at Jules, and then with a sigh he picked up the loupe and continued examining the coin in his hand. "A quarter is worth twenty-five cents."

"No, no," Jules said, shaking his head. "I meant a specific coin. Here." He placed the gold coin on top of the counter, where it made a heavy thud.

That got the man's attention. This time he put down both his coin and the loupe, and he reached for the gold coin. "Hmm," he said in an authoritative tone. "Heavy." He flicked at it with a pen knife, leaving a deep scratch. "Solid gold throughout. Where did you get this, young man?"

So it was real gold after all. "I found it in my garden when I was planting seeds," Jules said, looking away. "Do you know what country it's from?"

"Europe, I suspect. Yes, they use gold coins like this in Europe. This writing, along the edge? European." The man picked up his loupe again, pressed it to his eye, and examined the coin more closely. After a moment, he placed the coin on a scale and made a few adjustments.

"This coin would be worth more in Europe." He mumbled something under his breath and jotted some figures down on a scrap of paper. "Twenty dollars. I will give you twenty dollars for this coin."

Twenty dollars was more money than Jules had ever had before. The old Jules wouldn't have been able to resist the thought of all the jellybeans he could purchase, but he wasn't going to be taken for a fool any more. He reached for the coin and turned to leave.

"Thank you," he said. "I think I'll try the store down the street now." He was referring to Arbuckle's Coins and Stamps, a small shop opposite the bakery.

The old man held up his hand in the universal sign of patience and wagged his head from side to side. "Did I say twenty dollars? I meant two hundred dollars. I'm always doing that, mixing up my twenties with my two hundreds."

Jules had weighed the coin on the bean counter at the store before leaving home, just in case it turned out to be genuine, and had taken the extra step of looking up the price of gold in the daily newspaper. If he had done the math correctly—no sure thing, he realized—the value of the gold in that coin was worth at least three hundred and fifty dollars. He understood, though, that the last thing he needed was a bunch of nosy people prying about, trying to figure out where he had obtained it.

"I have some more planting to do in my garden during the summer," he mentioned casually. "It's possible I'll find even more coins buried there. If you'll give me two fifty, I'll make sure to bring any others here, too."

The old man thought for a minute. "At that price, this coin is not worth my trouble," he said. Then, when Jules turned to leave once more, the man quickly continued, "but I have an interest in European coins. You seem like a good boy. Just be sure to bring the others to me, too."

He opened the register, removed a stack of bills, and counted out the agreed-upon sum. "Remember," he added, "bring your other coins to *me*, not Arbuckle. Arbuckle won't be able to match this price, not worth your time and trouble to even mention this to him."

Jules nodded. Pleased with himself, he shoved the bills into his pocket, waved happily, and skipped out the door, heading for home.

Jules's mother hadn't returned, and the note was still right where he had left it. Now he was beginning to get concerned. Other than short trips to the grocery, his mother rarely left the house to begin with; an absence this long was almost unimaginable. Not knowing what to do, Jules went back into the store, sat down in the high stool behind the counter, and waited for a customer to appear. Before long, though, an unnaturally deep exhaustion came over him, and his eyelids began to droop. Soon he had fallen asleep with his head on top of the counter.

Eventually—he didn't know how much time had passed—he was woken by a gentle tug on his sleeve. He opened his eyes and began to exclaim, "There you are, Mom!" when he realized it wasn't his mother at all. It was the little troll, Bergen, wearing the same burlap tunic as before. Night had fallen; the only light in the store was the moonlight streaming through one of the windows.

"Everyone's glad that you came to the meetin' last night," the little troll said as Jules fumbled for a candle. "I was gettin' worried when you didn't show up at first, but better late than not at all, or so they say."

"I'm glad I came, too," Jules said with a yawn. He flicked a match and an amber glow filled the room. "It was quite exciting, although to be honest, I was a bit scared when I first walked down those stairs into the basement."

"You, scared! Ha! I can't imagine you bein' afraid of nothin.'"

"If you only knew."

Bergen shrugged. "Everyone took a real likin' to you. In fact, after you fell asleep, a large part of the discussion was about you."

"Is that so?" Jules replied. "What did they say?"

"Just this and the other thing."

"I think the phrase is 'this and that.'"

Bergen shrugged. "I like my way better; it has more panache."

"What does that mean, exactly?"

"Verve. Élan." Then, when Jules looked at him with a blank expression, the troll rolled his eyes and added, "flair," while muttering something under his breath about 'children,' 'education,' and 'these days' that Jules couldn't completely make out.

"Oh. Regardless, there's something about them I don't completely trust, and hearing that they were talking about me behind my back just makes it worse."

"It wasn't behind your back. You were layin' asleep right there in the same room."

"It's the same thing, and you know it."

"Is not. It was yer own fault for fallin' asleep before the meetin' was over."

"*Regardless*, Jules said, quite exasperated by the direction the discussion had taken, "it seemed like they all knew more about me than I do myself, like they've been secretly following me or something. Besides, they didn't seem interested when I offered to help. Sometimes I've got really good ideas, even though I'm just a kid."

"I'm sure that's true," Bergen said, "but you've been more than enough help already."

"That sounds a lot like what adults say when they are trying to get me to leave."

"Still, it's true."

To Jules, that made little sense. What had he done except crashed a private meeting, gazed at a strange holographic map, and fallen asleep? "I meant what I said in the woods," he said, changing the subject. "You're always welcome to return to purchase more coffee beans. And, if you want, you can have another burlap sack to make into a shirt. That one is starting to look a little worn, I'm sorry to say."

The troll squealed with delight. "Are you sure your mother wouldn't mind?"

"My mother—oh, no. She hasn't been home at all, not since last night. She was sleeping in her room when I left for your meeting, and I haven't seen her since. I'm really getting worried. She's never away for this long."

"Perhaps she came home while you were dozin' behind the counter and is back asleep in her bed."

"I guess so," Jules answered, though he doubted she would have let him sleep when there were still chores to be done. "Maybe we should check, just to make sure."

Together Jules and Bergen passed through the hall toward the master bedroom. Holding the candle above his head, Jules pushed the door open and peeked inside, quietly so as not to wake her. The caution was unnecessary; his mother wasn't there. Moreover, the room was a terrible mess. The bedspread was crumpled on the floor, and the blankets were piled in the center of the bed, as if she had gotten up in the middle of the night and had run out in fright.

"I've never seen her room like this," Jules said. He glanced at her nightstand, where a half-dozen small plastic cannisters were lined up in a row. One of the containers had been knocked over; tiny red and blue pills were scattered across the carpet beside her bed. "She usually keeps her things neat."

"Have you noticed your mother actin' at all strange recently?" Bergen asked. "Anythin' out of the ordinary could be a clue as to what might've happened to her."

Jules shut his eyes tight and thought hard about the past several months. "Well . . . for one thing, she hasn't seemed well," he answered. "I think she might be sick."

This remark surprised Jules, because before he said it out loud, he hardly noticed it was true. But as he thought about it, he realized she had recently seemed different somehow, ever since his father's death, in fact. *Getting old* was how he always thought of it, but now he had a strange feeling in the pit of his stomach that it was something entirely different. The best word he could think of was *deteriorating*, like the lands Thisted had described the previous night.

"What do you think could have happened to her?" he asked. "Do you think she's in any trouble?"

"Unfortunately, I don't have any trainin' in psychoanalysis, other than the usual kind that comes from readin' comics inside bubble-gum wrappers. But don't worry, boy. We'll get to the bottom of things." Then, after making Jules promise to go to bed, the little troll pledged to "see what he could find out" and return in the morning.

"You're a good friend," said Jules, glad to have someone to help him through this difficult period. And he meant it, too.

The following morning there was still no sign of Jules's mother, and her room was still in the same unkempt state. Jules was distressed. Other than for short trips to the store, his mother had never left him alone before, not even for a few hours. Where could she be? Could she really be in some sort of trouble?

"Something's going on," Jules said aloud. "And I wouldn't be at all surprised if those nasty-looking creatures from the Klepner basement were smack in the middle of it."

His suspicions had begun to rise and were nearly at the breaking point. By now he had half a mind to storm back over there and demand some answers. But after thinking about it for a few minutes, he realized the pointlessness of this. The creatures would just laugh at him, maybe insult him, too. Besides, they were unlikely to still be in the basement, and probably had gone back to wherever it was they had come from in the first place. He might as well face facts: he didn't know where his mother was, didn't know when she would return, and had no idea how to find out. Not knowing what else to do, he reentered the store, climbed up on the stool behind the counter, and vowed to wait patiently for Bergen's return, no matter how long it took. Maybe the little troll would have some answers. Before much time had passed, he felt himself nodding off.

"I don't know why I feel so drained," he said, trying to shake some life into his hands and fingers. "Still, a short nap couldn't hurt." Giving in to his exhaustion, he put his head down on the countertop.

A short time later he was roused by a mad tinkling of the doorbells. Jules jolted awake. "Good morning!" he called, rubbing the sleep from his eyes, expecting to see the first customer of the day.

"Good morning, glad t' meetcha an' all that," Bergen replied with a low bow. For of course it was just the little woodland troll, but this time he was leading two stout creatures, who looked every bit out of place as a pair of cows sunning at the beach. Each were roughly five feet tall and as round around their middles as wine barrels. "I've brought you some help."

"Help with what?"

"Well, with everythin', of course! Let me introduce to you Algard and his brother, Alesund. I'm sure you remember them from the meetin' two nights ago."

The two identical-looking creatures stepped forward and bowed low in unison. They were both dressed in silver shirts with broad, leather belts. "They're gnomes," Bergen continued, "and are descendants of the great gnome kings of old, so mind yer manners! Anyways, they can pass for humans in a pinch, and have offered their assistance to help you run things until yer mum returns from wherever she's gotten herself to."

"Hi," Jules said shyly, not sure how to address them, never having met royalty before. He bowed, then curtsied, and then out of an abundance of caution attempted both simultaneously, nearly losing his balance. "Don't just stand there like wallflowers!" he said, once he had regained his composure. "Come in and look around. Have either of you ever managed a store before?"

"Hmm, hmm, not exactly," one of the gnomes replied— which one, Jules wasn't sure. "Perhaps, hmm, hmm, you might give us some pointers."

Jules had never taught anyone anything in his entire life, and he didn't know where to start. It would be difficult enough to explain to people, but two gnomes? Would they even understand the difference between a lima bean and a string bean? He might as well try to teach an octopus how to knit a sweater. Jules decided to begin by identifying each item displayed for sale. When the gnomes seemed to have that down, Jules continued, "Now, let's go over prices. Those coffee beans, they're three dollars a pound."

When one of the gnomes responded, "What's a dollar?" Jules realized this would be harder than expected. As he was patiently describing the difference between a dime and a quarter, Bergen suddenly started hopping up and down and desperately waving his arms.

"Someone's coming," the troll exclaimed.

Sure enough, the sound of muffled speech could be heard through the closed door and was getting louder. Whoever it was, they were coming up the walk! "Uh oh," Jules said, not sure what to do. "Bergen, you better get out of sight."

Bergen sprinted over to the corner, leaped high in the air, and dove deep into one of the vats of coffee beans as if he were a skin diver searching for clams at the sea bottom. A moment later his eyes and nose popped up, but the rest of him remained submerged.

Before Alesund could find a decent hiding spot, Jules grabbed the gnome by the arm and led him into the middle of the room. "You'll have to get used to dealing with human customers sooner or later," he said. "Now's as good a time as any." Turning to Algard he added, "The way the two of you look so much alike, you should probably get out of sight. I think I can pass one of you off as human, but not both at the same time. Too suspicious. Try and hide somewhere, and don't stay out in the open like that! Don't want customers to think something strange is going on."

But it was too late, for just then the door opened, and in walked Mr. and Mrs. Bottomsley along with their daughter Betsy. A clove of garlic hung around Betsy's neck by a thin cotton string, and she looked quite unhappy about it.

"Hello, Jules," Mrs. Bottomsley said. "Is your mother here? We'd like to purchase some things this morning. Go find her, that's a good child." She was a tall, haughty woman, and spoke in a low-pitched throaty voice.

Mr. Bottomsley, an overweight man who always had a peculiar look on his face that suggested he would prefer to be somewhere else, stood by the door, as if he was afraid to come all the way inside. He carefully eyed Algard, who stood near the door frozen in place, staring straight ahead without moving a muscle.

"No, Ma'am," Jules answered, feeling quite nervous. "She's not. I can help you, though."

"Very well," Mrs. Bottomsley said. "I'd like three pounds of lima beans, two pounds of string beans, five pounds of bean sprouts, and twelve cans of bean paste. Move about it, young man, we are in a bit of a hurry this morning; we are taking Betsy to the circus."

Betsy smiled broadly from behind her mother's dress and then wandered off to explore the store.

"This is my Uncle, uh, Al," Jules said, shoving Alesund forward with such force that the gnome collided with Mrs. Bottomsley, knocking her purse to the floor. "My mother . . . uh . . . she went on vacation, and he's going to help me watch the store while she's away."

"A fine idea, a fine idea," Mrs. Bottomsley muttered, retrieving her bag while noticeably trying to keep her temper in check. "A boy such as you couldn't possibly be expected to do everything around here all by yourself."

"*No, shake her hand, shake her hand,*" Jules implored quietly, stopping Alesund mid-bow. The gnome tentatively grasped the woman's fingers, which she had held out to him, and shook them vigorously until she pulled her hand away in alarm.

"Well!" Mrs. Bottomsley said. "Nice to meet you too, I'm sure!"

As Jules fetched a pair of paper bags and began collecting and weighing the requested items, Mrs. Bottomsley attempted to start a conversation. "You say you're the boy's uncle?"

"No, I didn't," Alesund stammered. "I'm a gnome, you know. A gnome." He pronounced the first letter separately from the rest of the word, so it sounded like "guh-nome."

Uh-oh. Jules cringed. *That did it.* From across the store, he winced, waiting for the inevitable aftermath of this admission.

"I see," Mrs. Bottomsley replied, not missing a beat. "Is that anything like a biologist?"

"Not really, no."

"I have a friend who is married to a chemist," Mrs. Bottomsley continued, seeming happy to find someone to talk at. "A brilliant man. Sure to win the Nobel Prize someday." She proceeded to describe this man's work and her friend's marital difficulties in excruciating detail, while Alesund pretended to pay attention, interjecting "oh, really?" and "is that so?" every so often at not completely inappropriate times, to Jules's everlasting relief.

As they continued their idle chatter, Betsy wandered around the floor and eventually reached the corner containing the barrels filled with coffee beans. As she peeked behind them, there was a sudden movement from inside the nearest vat, and Bergen popped his head out and took a nibble from the clove of garlic, which at that moment had been hanging by the string right over his head. Almost immediately he put his hand over his mouth in alarm, realizing his error. "Sorry," he said between mouthfuls, before ducking his head back under the cover of beans.

Betsy giggled. "You're cute," she said, poking at him with her tiny fingers. "Can you play with me?"

Bergen popped his head up again and winked. "Shhh. I'm playing 'Hide and Go Tag' with the others," he said quietly. "Don't give me away, okay?"

"Okay," Betsy said.

"Come now, hurry up with that order, Jules," called Mrs. Bottomsley, having clearly tired of her conversation with this odd Uncle Al. "Mr. Bottomsley is getting antsy." Mr. Bottomsley was, in fact, not getting antsy at all, but was closely examining the stationary gnome by the door, peeking over to stare at Alesund from time to time. As Jules watched, Mr. Bottomsley stuck his index finger deep into Algard's right ear and twisted it back and forth a few times.

"Fascinating," Mr. Bottomsley mumbled.

By now Jules had finished collecting the items. "That will be fourteen gold pieces," he said before he could stop himself. "Dollars, I meant dollars," he corrected. "Fourteen dollars."

"Gold pieces, that's very funny, young man," Mrs. Bottomsley replied. "That's quite an imagination you have! Better do something to correct that. Children who invent nonsense don't grow up to become responsible adults, you know." She then turned to Betsy, who had returned to her side. "Don't ever let your imagination run away from you like that, Betsy. You must always act like a grownup." She took a close look. "What happened to your garlic? It looks like there's a piece missing."

"A little man jumped out of the barrel and ate it," Betsy replied.

"*Betsy!*" Mrs. Bottomsley cried. "Don't make up stories. It's bad for my complexion. We're going straight home. No circus for you today."

"But—"

"Not another word, young lady."

Betsy exhaled hard and glanced at the barrel, where Bergen stuck his head up and mouthed the word 'sorry.'

As they were leaving, Jules heard Mr. Bottomsley exclaim, "Did you see the garden gnome by the door? What fantastic workmanship! It looks just like the boy's uncle."

To which Mrs. Bottomsley replied, "It gives me the willies. Garden gnomes belong outside in the garden, not inside the home. That's why they are called garden gnomes. Betsy," she continued, "Always remember that lawn ornaments belong on the lawn, not in the house."

"Okay," Betsy replied as the door finally shut behind them.

"Whew!" said Jules, when all was clear. "That was close." He reached into the barrel of cinnamon-flavored coffee beans and pulled Bergen out by the scruff of the neck. "There'll be no more of that!" he said to his little friend, who was now covered in a light brown dust and nearly intoxicated from the pungent aroma.

Algard shook his head vigorously from side-to-side and stretched his muscles. "A garden gnome, indeed!" he said. "Ridiculous."

CHAPTER 6

Answers

Within a short time, Alesund was managing the store as if born for it. He ordered new goods and supplies when needed, and even negotiated a special volume discount from McAllister so Jules no longer had to manually sort the coffee beans by their aroma. The gnome had a natural talent for accounting and recordkeeping, which was a great relief to Jules, who could never understand all the columns of numbers and figures without earning a terrific headache from his effort. People began to notice how well the store was run, and Jules had never seen so many customers. They filled their bags with beans, admiring the selection and wondering aloud why they had never previously done their shopping there. Some asked Jules about his mother in hushed tones, as if they were afraid to pose the question. At such times, he'd just respond that she was on vacation, thank you very much, and would be back soon, next week most probably, and if not by then surely not long thereafter. But from the way they looked at him from a distance and shook their heads, he grasped that they didn't believe him in the slightest.

After midnight things really got busy, for that's when Jules unlatched the front door to a steady parade of trolls, gnomes, frites, and other creatures of the forest. They came with harps and flutes and they sang and danced until dawn. They told stories, too, wonderful stories of trolls that ate evil knights or gnomes that rescued children from wicked witches. And they ate beans, lots and lots of beans, for which they paid with more of those pretty gold coins. Some of these Jules sold to the old man in the coin shop and used the money to purchase more inventory, but mostly he kept them for himself, just in case a time someday came when he would need them.

The gnomes Alesund and Algard agreed that the sight of both of them at the same time might attract the wrong kind of attention from human customers, and thus made a great effort not to be seen together. So while Alesund greeted the customers and rang up their orders, his brother remained in the back, cooking meals and generally ensuring the house was in order. Despite Algard's curious tendency to garnish the sandwiches with leaves and a few long blades of grass, there was no question that Jules was now eating better than he had in years, and after just a few weeks he had already begun to fill out around the middle and grow noticeably taller.

In this way the days and weeks slowly passed. The air turned hot and sticky, as it did every summer, and Jules's life settled into a routine of sorts. Of Bergen Jules saw nothing, not even at the midnight gatherings. Jules made it a habit to leave a handful of coffee beans on the counter in case Bergen reappeared with news about his mother, but each morning the pile was untouched. Yet Jules never stopped wondering what had happened to his mother and when she would return—and if the two gnomes knew anything about it, they never let on.

On this particular morning, Jules had been left alone and in charge of things for a few hours while the gnomes separately ran various errands around town, when he noticed a small piece of paper on the floor, hidden partway under the counter. The edges were ragged, and it looked like it had been torn from a notebook and ripped in half. It must have slipped off the countertop by accident and fallen there where it wouldn't be noticed. Jules reached down, intending to throw the scrap in the trash, and discovered to his surprise that there was some writing on it.

Perhaps it was a note from his mother. He snatched the page off the floor.

The message was written in an ugly scrawl. At first glance, it appeared to be nonsense, just a collection of lines and squiggles. But after staring at the scrap of paper for a few moments, he began to recognize that they were words after all, just in a strange script that was difficult to read. He worked on each letter and after a few minutes was able to work it out.

"Jules," the note began. "I have important news about you-know-what. Come to the meeting house when you get this." Between blots of ink it was signed, Bergen.

"I wonder how long that's been there?" He exhaled hard. "Just like that silly little troll to leave a note where it could fall out of sight, and without putting a time or date on it! Especially if it's as important as he's making it out to be. Well, what's done is done, and if he's been waiting for me long, it's nothing but his own fault!"

But there was no reason to keep Bergen waiting any more than necessary, especially if the news was about his mother. He grabbed his light jacket and the old fedora from the coat rack, flipped the sign in the window to "closed" and sprinted down the road as fast as he could, not bothering with the dirt path. When he reached the Klepner house, he slipped inside through the still-unlocked front door, careful to check that no one was passing by who might notice him trespassing on private property and call the authorities.

Jules shut the door behind him, hardly taking the time to notice how different the living room looked with sunlight flowing through the windows. He pounced down the stairs two steps at a time, nearly tripping on a loose shoelace before bursting into the basement.

"I'm here, Berg—" he began, and then stopped short.

For the room was filled once again with most of the same group of creatures who were at the meeting held here weeks earlier (minus Alesund and Algard, of course). They were all standing or wandering around the room aimlessly, as though waiting for something to happen but weren't quite sure what it would be, or possibly waiting for something to stop happening that had already begun. The long table that was here previously was now gone, which made the room feel less cramped and provided enough room for the strange creatures to mill about. Thisted was here too, but the enormous mountain troll was far too large to do anything but sit on the floor with his knees pulled up to his chest.

The room was brighter now, courtesy of a few small casement windows high up on the walls that were just above ground level and obscured from outside the house by a row of overgrown bushes. Now that he could see clearly, Jules noticed the room was unfinished; a bare concrete floor spanned the length of the room, bordered by cinderblock walls with wood struts nailed across them horizontally. In the far corner of the room, a large oval-shaped hole had been carved through the wall, forming the mouth of a tunnel that quite evidently stretched far underground.

"So that's how they come and go," Jules muttered. "I wonder where it leads. Probably into the forest or some other such place, I imagine."

But Jules did not think any more about it, for his eyes then fell on something else in the room, something terrible and disturbing that took his breath away.

It was a woodland troll, wearing a fancy blue tunic with ornate gold trim, although the shirt was badly soiled and torn in two or three spots. The little troll was obviously injured, and horribly so. It lay on a bed made of grass and leaves. A tiny fiddle rested at its side, its fingerboard snapped in two. Jules noticed the troll's forehead was wrapped with bandages, as was its left arm, right hand and right leg. Although moaning in pain, it was watching Jules intently through deep, brown eyes. Bergen was at the injured troll's side, applying a cold compress to its head and trying to provide comfort.

"Is he all right?" Jules asked. "What happened?"

"I think," said Hortlax, with a serious expression on his face, "that it is time we explained things to the boy. After this *development*, it is important that he know the whole story—or at least the important parts of it, at any rate."

"Very well," Thisted agreed, as the other creatures nodded and murmured to each other. In the natural light the gigantic troll somehow didn't seem quite as menacing. He sighed slowly, as if he wasn't sure where to start, or even what language to speak in.

Thisted began, "When you were here before, all those weeks ago, we showed you a map of our world. Do you remember?"

"How could I ever forget?" Jules responded. "It was beautiful. I've never seen anything like it."

"Nor will you ever again. It is the only one like it. That is more than a map of our world. Our world, you see, is a reflection of the map."

"The map is the world, and the world is the map," explained a cave troll named Larvik, not really explaining anything. "It's quite simple, really."

"It's known as the Map of Eternity," Thisted continued. "It is a very powerful thing, and it is what binds our world together. It is a hard thing to describe. Our world and the Map are the same, in a sense."

"But isn't that usually the case when it comes to maps?" Jules asked. "At least with regard to the better-made ones."

"Not like this. You see—"

"Think of it this way," Hortlax said, blowing a soap-bubble out of a hole at the top of his head. "When you looked at the map, you saw things, well, *move*, if you will."

"I do remember," Jules recalled. "I thought I saw mist rising from a huge waterfall. And at one point, it looked as if a great flock of birds was flying over the land."

"And so they were, at that very moment."

"So I wasn't imagining it!"

"No, I should say not," Hortlax replied. "Some things, such as your waterfall, the flock of birds, boats on a river—these can be seen quite clearly. Other objects are smaller and harder to notice. If you had a strong enough magnifying glass, and pointed it at the right place, you might even see people and creatures wandering about. Those things are all actually happening in our world as you see them on the map. It's like a witch's magic looking-glass from a fairy tale, although on a map instead of inside a mirror."

"Much more mobile that way," added a river-troll named Rindal, who had become a frequent visitor to the store. "You could hardly lug a mirror around with you while tramping around the forest, you know. They're highly impracticable, when you get right down to it."

"But our world does not last forever," Thisted continued. "It thrives for a long time, until after several decades it begins to weaken and die, just like any animal, bird, or tree. Or a human," he added as an afterthought, looking directly at Jules. "Gradually it begins to go through changes, terrible changes. Trees lose their foliage and wither. Deserts expand and swallow up entire towns and villages. Even mountains crumble and the ground tears apart, creating great rifts in the earth through which escape poisonous steam and gas."

"But if your land has gone through this before," Jules said, "there obviously must be a way to stop the deterioration, even reverse it. Right?"

"That's very perceptive," Thisted said. "But no, there is no way to stop it, or even to reverse the damage. Instead, a new world must be created to take the place of the old one. The new world will have different mountain ranges, perhaps a swamp where the old world had a desert, perhaps features that we can't even imagine. Great civilizations will vanish, to be replaced by other cultures, equally special and unique. The old towns and villages will disappear, as if they never existed; and replaced by new cities, whose inhabitants have no knowledge of what came before them and who think that they have been there all along. We call this process the 'Reformation.' Are you grasping this? It is like a phoenix rising from the ashes, if you understand that sort of imagery."

"I'm not sure," Jules said. "It makes me think of the school blackboard, when Ms. Binkley wipes it clean with the eraser just so she can just write different equations on it."

"That is an apt analogy."

Jules bit his lip in thought. "But if all that is true—that everything in the forest vanishes during this time—then why are all of you still here? Begging your pardon, but why didn't you vanish, too? Not that I don't like you or anything like that," he added hastily.

"Ah," Hortlax said. "A fine question. The races of trolls and gnomes and frites have existed long before Mankind. We once lived openly among you, but we have since been pushed into the dark and secret corners of the earth. Although we reside within those lands, we are merely travelers, interlopers. We are thus unaffected by these world-changes, as any human would be who happened to be inside the forest during one of these transitions. Continuing to exist as before, but with everything changed around them."

"Not the safest place to be," Rindal interjected. "Can you imagine standing around in the middle of a field when it suddenly turns to a marsh?"

"A lava field."

"Quicksand."

"The middle of a stampeding herd of tri-horned bison."

"A sun-drenched island with unlimited fruity drinks. And a hammock strung between two palm trees, with all the berries a troll could—"

All the creatures turned to glare at Bergen. "What? A troll can dream, can't he? Why do you all have to be so negative all the time? Sheesh."

When the predictable shouts and catcalls finally quieted down, Jules asked, "So how does this world of yours change?"

"The key is the Map of Eternity," the mountain troll answered quietly, drawing out each syllable. The windows vibrated from his rumbling voice. "When our world is dying, as it is now—or perhaps I should say as it was then—we are tasked with seeking out a human child to gaze upon the Map with open mind and open heart." Thisted shut his eyes and continued in an even softer voice. "When a human child looks upon the Map, our world is recreated anew. Reformed. We have no control over what will happen, no knowledge of what our world will become. Neither does the chosen child; and, in fact, it is imperative that the child *not* know what he or she has been called upon to do, so his or her mind is clear. Somehow—and this is beyond our understanding—the Map detects what is in the child's heart and within his or her thoughts, and from this a new world is created.

"I know what you are thinking, Jules. All we needed to do was pick a child and our problem would be solved. Well, it is not that simple. You see, the choice of child is very important, for we have but one chance to get it right. For once a child looks at the Map during the Time of Deterioration, there is no going back. The process cannot be stopped: a new world will be formed, and we are stuck with what we have, for better or for worse, until the cycle starts over again.

"The last time we chose well; the previous human selected to look at the Map, many years ago, was a romantic at heart. For the past several decades we have lived in a world of knights and dragons, and castles, and brave heroes that traveled the land on valiant quests for nothing but the hands of the women they love. Before that, unfortunately, the human child we chose did not have much love in her heart or any imagination to speak of, and our world was a small, dark place." He shuddered at what was evidently a powerful memory. "We chose poorly, and our world became a harsh wasteland that could barely support life."

"You chose me this time!" Jules exclaimed with sudden realization. "I looked at the Map. Did I reform your world? Is that what you are saying?"

"Yes, Jules. When Hortlax opened the Map of Eternity and you looked upon it, you wiped away our existing but decaying world and recreated it anew from nothingness."

"Is that why the Map appeared to grow more and more into focus the longer I looked at it?"

"Yes," the mountain troll continued. "It takes several minutes for the Reformation to be complete. You probably did not notice, but for a split second after the map was uncovered, it was a blank slate, just a template. Then, as the Map caught hold of your heart and internal energies, it slowly grew and formed the patterns and images that you saw rise from its pages. Gradually and simultaneously our world changed, too, until it matched the features splayed across the Map. Now our world is filled with forests and great deserts, magnificent cities, new and exotic species, ancient civilizations—all things that didn't exist before that night other than deep in the recesses of your mind.

"Usually, we have advance notice of when the current world cycle is ending, and we have enough time to identify a suitable human child to gaze upon the Map. This time, however, the Deterioration began unexpectedly and took all of us by surprise, and we were left scrambling. We searched for several years to no avail, for we were unable to locate a human child whom we could trust with this task. The current crop of children," he said with a sad look on his face, "is unimaginative and coldhearted."

"Too much television and video games," interjected Larvik, "and not enough book reading."

"The legends say that if the Deterioration is allowed to progress too far without a child gazing upon the Map, the forest world will fade away forever," Thisted continued. "I was afraid we had reached that point! It was only at the last moment, when we were about to admit our failure and wait for the inevitable result, that the woodland troll, Bergen, nominated you, and the rest you know."

"So that explains why the world reflected in the Map looked so full of life, despite your insistence that your world was melting away to nothingness. It had already been rebuilt as soon as I looked at it."

"Yes."

"But why are you telling me all of this? I thought Bergen asked me to come back here because he had found out something about my mother. Haven't you learned what has happened to her yet? She still hasn't returned, and it's been weeks and weeks since she disappeared."

"Hmmm, yes," Thisted said, fidgeting uneasily. "I was just coming to that. As you can probably imagine, a map that has the ability to reveal what is happening anywhere in the world would be quite valuable. Dangerous, too. Why, if the Map were to fall into the wrong hands . . ."

". . . and?"

"Someone apparently wants the Map of Eternity very badly. Your mother, you see, has been kidnapped, and the kidnapper has made it quite clear that he will only release her in exchange for the Map itself."

CHAPTER 7

Setting Off

Kidnapped . . . The word echoed through his mind. Like he was poisoned, Jules suddenly felt physically ill and sensed himself growing faint. As he slipped to the floor, he was dimly aware of hands pressing against his arms and back, trying desperately to prop him up. The whole thing was unbelievable. His mother, kidnapped? She wasn't anyone special, certainly not anyone rich or famous. Who would want to kidnap her? He wanted to scream but couldn't open his mouth.

Images flashed through his mind. He remembered a time when he was five, and his parents took him to the annual spring festival in the grassy park near the lake. That day there was a kite-flying contest. Kites shaped like dragons looped overhead and were directed to perform tricks through tugs on their strings. Later that afternoon, his father bought a diamond-shaped one and taught him how to fly it. He remembered how he ran across the cool grass on bare feet, dragging the kite behind him, until a sudden gust of wind sent it soaring to join the dozens of others already there, like a baby bird learning to use its wings. It was glorious. He looked at his parents with pride. They were sitting together on the grass, holding hands and beaming back at him. He felt as though he could do anything, accomplish anything. It was one of his best memories, one of his few remaining memories of the way things used to be. And now his father was dead, and his mother was . . . was what, exactly? Where was she? Who had taken her? Why?

He heard voices and tried to focus. He opened his eyes and realized he had been lying on the floor. Bergen was standing on his chest, slapping him on the cheek in an effort to wake him. A frite he recognized as Kalix was standing over his body, looking at him anxiously; it must've been Kalix's elongated hands he had felt on his arms and back when he collapsed. Jules moved Bergen to the floor next to him and sat up gingerly.

"What happened?" he gasped.

"You fainted," Kalix said. "You were out for just a moment. It was a physical reaction to—"

"No, not me. My mother. Tell me what happened to her. Don't leave anything out. I want to know the truth. The *whole* truth this time, without any riddles or confusing talk."

"It was the count, of course," said Kalix, stroking his thick beard with his long fingers and getting them momentarily tangled in the strands. "Count Barchmod. But I'm sure you've guessed that by now."

"I don't know who that is."

"Count Barchmod is an evil sorcerer who wishes to rule over us all," Larvik said gravely, his low voice honking like an out-of-tune saxophone. "He resides in a great castle deep in the forest-world, a fortress called Pho Altis that is impossible to enter and harder to leave."

Jules's head was still foggy, and he was having trouble following this conversation. An evil sorcerer . . . it was surreal, almost as if he had stepped into the very pages of one of the fairy-book stories that lined the shelves of his father's dusty bookcases. He held out his arm, and Kalix helped him to his feet. "What does he want with my mother?"

"Not your mother, Jules," Kalix said. "She is only a pawn to him, to be traded for something more valuable: the Map of Eternity. With the Map in his grasp, no one would be able to withstand his forces, for it would enable him to locate and destroy those who dare resist him. He's been trying to get his hands on the Map for a long, long time, and it looks like now he's stumbled on a scheme that may work."

"A—a long time?" Jules stuttered. "Now that doesn't make any sense. Why didn't this count person and his castle disappear when I looked at the Map? I thought you said everything in the forest vanished, like it never existed. Is he like you, a troll or a gnome, who isn't affected by the Map at all?"

There was a pause. "No, he's not like us, Jules," Thisted said. "In fact, he's not from the forest-world at all. He's from yours."

"You mean he's—"

"Human," finished Larvik. "Just like you."

Jules reeled. A *human* had kidnapped his mother? He thought again of some of the stories his father had told him, tales about people who had gone to live in the forest, away from civilization, and how many of them were criminals or outlaws.

Reitan, a river troll with paddle-like hands, spoke now. "Many years ago, the count left your world and took refuge in the forest. Of course, he wasn't known as Count Barchmod then. He took that name later, as his power grew. He built the White Fortress using rock and stone he carried with him, and named it Pho Altis, the Fortress of Eternal Light. That it was constructed with foreign materials is why it was not erased during this or any previous Reformation.

"Over the years he became strong and attracted many followers, until two decades ago, he attempted to hold power over the entire forest-world. For years the lands were engulfed in a terrible war."

"Well—what happened?" Jules asked. "He didn't win, did he?"

"Thankfully, no," Thisted said. "The count seized control of much of the forest-world, but a small pocket of resistance held strong against him in a single great kingdom. The battle waged for weeks. Eventually the count abducted the daughter of the monarch, the Copper Princess, and imprisoned her in a tower, thinking that would break the resolve of those fighting against him. But this act had the opposite effect, and the people of the city fought with renewed vigor. In the end, the count was defeated through the courage of another human, the one who preceded you, Jules, as the previous Map-Gazer. By then he was no longer a child, but a full-grown man, but he returned and came to our aid when most needed. He entered our world, freed the princess and overthrew Count Barchmod. The count escaped and took refuge at Pho Altis, where he has remained, awaiting his revenge.

"But there was a cost," Thisted continued. "During that battle, the count first became aware of the existence of the Map of Eternity, for it was used to defeat him. Through that knowledge, he now understood his battle for control of the forest was ultimately doomed to fail, for eventually the next Reformation would occur, and in an instant he would lose all the power he had worked so hard to gain. He knew then that in order to retain control and rule over these lands forever, he would have to possess the Map itself. Since then, he has been plotting to obtain it for himself."

"I guess this guy is pretty dangerous," Jules said. The talk about the Copper Princess and her abduction long ago made him think of his mother. "How was my mother captured?" he asked. "And why did this count bother kidnapping her at all? If he was just interested in getting the Map for himself, he could have left her alone, and simply tried to steal the Map during the council meeting."

"We think that was his original intent," Hortlax said. "He sent two of his men through the forest, with designs to interrupt the Council, seize the Map, and kidnap *you* at the same time. *You* would be taken to Pho Altis, where the count would force you to reform the world in his presence. Then he would have the new Map to himself, and with it, unlimited power over the new forest-world and the key to dominating it. But they were too late, you see, and the world changed around them while they were still on their journey, quite near to where we are right now. Unexpectedly, then, they stumbled upon your mother, who was wandering the forest alone, and they devised a new, more sinister plan."

"Oh, she must have been out looking for me!" Jules cried. "She must've woken and noticed I wasn't home. So this is my fault."

"Regret is pointless," Kalix said. "It is what it is. These are brutal, vicious men. They would have done anything to get hold of the Map, even kill us all."

"How do you know all this? Why didn't you tell me before?"

"We haven't been keeping things from you, Jules," Thisted said, "if that's what you are asking. We only just found out ourselves, from that injured woodland troll. We stumbled upon him yesterday, and in bits and pieces he told us what had happened, how a pair of men riding on stallions with coats as black as coal appeared in the forest and took your mother away that night."

Something rang in Jules's memory. "Horses? You know, I think I might've seen it happen when I was first looking at the Map. I thought I saw something moving in the woods near my house, but I didn't think anything of it."

"That was undoubtedly what you were seeing, Jules," Thisted said. "To answer your question, this poor troll was captured with your mother, and brought with her to Pho Altis, released to deliver us the message that her freedom could be secured through an exchange for the Map. Since then, he's been trying to return as quickly as possible, and was injured terribly in the effort."

"His name is Bryggen," Bergen said. "He's one of my distant cousins, on my Mother's side of things. He's always been the adventurous one in the family."

Jules approached the injured troll, who was still lying on the grass bed, and addressed him for the first time. "Oh, please, if you are able to talk, tell me how my mother is! I must know more."

"Yer mum was doin' fine," Bryggen said, coughing, "at least as far as I could tell. A little scared. And who wouldn't be, for when we reached Pho Altis, 'twas none other than the count himself who met us at the gate."

"The count! What was he like?"

"He was dressed in a white robe, with white gloves on his hands. Around his neck hung a long silver necklace from which dangled a large circular silver medallion. But what I remember most was his eyes. They burned with an inner fire I've never seen in a human before.

"He grabbed yer mum by the arms and pulled her close to him. He looked her over, very carefully. Then he reached out with his gloved hands and began to poke and prod her in her stomach, mutterin' 'excellent,' and 'this will do quite nicely,' under his breath."

"Why would he do that?" demanded Jules, feeling sick. "What is he going to do with my mother?"

Reitan made a low sound from deep in his throat. "There have been stories—rumors, mostly, of things that occur deep within the bowels of the White Fortress," the river troll said. "Terrible things, evil things. Occasionally the local townspeople have heard screams coming from within the walls of that horrible place, screams of pain, of great hurt, of agony. No one is sure, but . . . we think the count has been performing experiments on all sorts of creatures—trolls, gnomes, even people. Medical experiments. To what end, no one knows. No one imprisoned in Pho Altis has ever been seen again."

Jules stared in shock as a wave of anger built up inside him, like bubbles trapped in a soda bottle getting shaken about. His mother was being treated like some animal. "We can't just leave her there. We have to free her. We have to give him the Map."

"If you wish to try to rescue her, that is your own business," Larvik said. "But the Map's fate isn't for you to decide. You must find another way to end her imprisonment."

Jules stomped around the room, waving his hands in frustration. "But without the Map, the count won't let her go! You *must* give it to me. We have to help her and end her suffering. It's the only way."

"We cannot allow it," Larvik countered. His eyes blazed as he spoke, and Jules had a fleeting glimpse of how dangerous these creatures could be if they put their minds to it. "Haven't you been listening to anything we've said? The Map is more important than any one person! The future of our world rests on its safety. We must protect it with our very lives. We cannot let a—a boy run off with it into the wild to simply hand it to someone intent on using it against us!"

"No!" Jules shouted. "That isn't true at all. None of that is true. My mother is more important than your stupid Map. I don't care about this world of yours, even if I did create it by accident. We have to rescue her."

The room erupted in argument.

"The boy recreated our world, and so the Map is his by right."

"The Map must be protected above all else."

"Let him rescue his mother another way."

"Maybe he could photograph the Map. The count would hardly know the difference."

"He's not an idiot."

"I think I could draw it on some parchment."

"We should play marbles for it."

"Darts."

"Tiddlywinks."

"Look," Jules said. The room slowly quieted down. "My mother needs my help. If I don't try to help her, I . . . I don't know what I'll do. I *have* to try. And trying means bringing the Map to the count. Maybe I can trick him in the end, find a way to get the Map back after he lets my Mom go. I don't know, but I do know I have to try." His eyes were watering and he sniffled abruptly. "I don't even have to hold it. The rest of you can keep it hidden away with you until we reach Pho Altis if you don't trust me. I don't know what will happen, but I do know that we have to try." The tears were coming now, large droplets running down his cheeks to the corners of his mouth. He looked imploringly at Thisted. "Please?"

There was a long moment of silence that hung heavy on the air. Finally the giant mountain troll spoke again. "Yes," Thisted said. "I agree with Jules. We must let him try. His mother must be rescued before things go any further."

"If the count were to get hold of the Map, his power would become unstoppable," Larvik countered. "You know this. It cannot be allowed. We cannot risk this."

"It is a risk," Thisted agreed. "But one that cannot be avoided. Without Jules's help, the forest-world would be facing destruction even now. Surely, we owe him our trust."

"Let him try to rescue his mother some other way," the cave troll grumbled. "Let him take a sword like one of the heroes of old."

"A slingshot."

"A battering ram."

"A catapult."

"A small battalion."

"Three canons and a regiment of horsemen."

"A Sherman tank."

"A laser pistol."

"A *what?*"

"Well, he'd have to invent it first, but the theoretical underpinnings behind it are sound."

"No, no," Thisted said. "None of those things will be helpful. The count is a very powerful man, and the fortress of Pho Altis well defended. I fear that all of those methods of attack would fail."

"Not the laser pistol. Just increase the setting."

Thisted waved for quiet. "We don't know what the future will bring. Perhaps the count will discover he is unable to access the magic that dwells within the Map, for there is a magic about it we don't fully understand. Or perhaps in the end Jules will discover a way to free his mother without surrendering it to him. At any rate, each of the previous Reformers have gone on a great quest, and perhaps this is to be Jules's."

The mountain troll turned to face Jules. "Very well. We've explained the consequences, told you what is at risk. It is your decision. You are as hardheaded as the last Map-Gazer, in your own way. We do not have the power to stop you. You may go."

The way Thisted looked at him made Jules realize he had horribly misunderstood things. "Wait," he protested. "You're all coming with me, right? Aren't you?"

Thisted smiled with only half an effort but didn't say anything.

Jules looked around the room, into the faces of the creatures he had begun to regard as friends, and he saw in their expressions kindness and hope even as they shook their heads. "But I need you," he pleaded. "All of you. I can't do this myself."

Thisted's smile widened. "Oh, no, not quite by yourself. You'll need someone to watch over you. And since the little woodland troll got you into this mess to begin with, I can think of nothing fairer than for him to accompany you."

Jules nearly exploded with joy. "Do you mean it? Hooray! Bergen, you're coming too!"

"Great," the little troll said with a sigh. "Just the sort of adventure I need."

"I'll be careful, I promise," said Jules, addressing the Council. "And if there's any way to save my mother without surrendering the Map, I'll try to do so, even though I'm just a boy."

"Just a boy?" Thisted said. "Oh, no; you are much, much more, but you will have to discover *that* by yourself."

"You'll need some way to travel there, of course," Hortlax said, blowing out another soap bubble. "The trip to Pho Altis will be long and treacherous. You can't go by foot."

"What you need," Reitan shouted, "is a chariot."

"Try to stay in this century, will you?" Larvik snorted. "What he really needs is a helicopter."

"A houseboat," Rindal said.

"A rocket ship," Hortlax offered.

"How about a sports coupe with a V6 turbocharged engine?" suggested Kalix, the frite. "You shouldn't travel at all unless you can travel in style."

"I'm afraid I don't have any of those things," Jules said, his laughter surprising him and breaking the tension. "Besides, I'm not old enough to drive. I think we'll have to walk, even if it takes the rest of the summer."

"Perhaps this will do," a familiar voice said. Standing in the corner were Alesund and Algard, who had entered the basement unnoticed. Between them they were holding a gleaming red bicycle. A pair of white streamers dangled from the handlebars and a wire basket hung over the front tire.

"Oh, it's perfect!" Jules said.

"A sports car would be faster," grumbled Kalix. "I'm sure the boy could learn to drive in no time—"

"Nevertheless, we must work with what we have," Thisted said. "Then everything is settled. You may leave immediately. Algard and Alesund will continue to watch the store in your absence. And mind you, try to stay safe! All sorts of dangers will be awaiting you once you enter the forest." Thisted gestured to Hortlax, who pulled the thick book from his pack and handed it to Jules. "Here is the Map. Study it carefully, because it will give you direction when you are lost, and with direction comes purpose. But whatever you do, do not reveal that you carry it with you, for there are many who covet it for themselves, and they will be searching for you."

"We've packed you some things," said Alesund, holding up Jules's backpack. "There are some extra clothes, and some energy bars, as well as a small retractable umbrella for nasty weather. There's also a notebook to jot down an account of your adventures. We'd love to hear about them when you get back."

"And some gold coins, too," Algard added. "You might need some money on your trip, and I've found that gold is an acceptable form of currency pretty much everywhere."

"But—"

"Bergen will help you with that along the way," Alesund said.

"But—"

"That too."

Jules didn't give up. "But—"

"Don't be such a worry wart."

"Remember," Hortlax said. "This is *your* adventure, and yours alone. No one can tell you what to do, or how to do it. Whether you succeed or fail is entirely up to you and your wits."

"An' me!" Bergen squeaked. "I'll help the boy as best I can."

"Good." Thisted nodded. "He will need plenty of help before this is all over."

"I—this is all so sudden. How do I start?" Jules asked. "Which way do I go?"

"Just step through the tunnel," Thisted answered, indicating the hole carved in the wall. "That's all you need to do. And then follow the road. Good luck, Jules, and try to remember everything we've told you."

"I will. Goodbye, everyone!"

And with Bergen scampering at his side, six steps to every one of his, Jules crossed the room and entered the tunnel, pulling the bicycle alongside. The tunnel was dark and smelled like raw cabbage. As he advanced, he felt a strong vibration in the earth through his shoes. Once, he looked back to see if his friends were still watching him, but the tunnel had turned and they were out of sight.

"Just what sort of mess have you gotten us into now," he heard Bergen grumble from down near his feet.

Jules reached down in the darkness and lifted the troll to his shoulder, where the troll sat with his legs dangling over Jules's collarbone. "We'll be all right," he whispered. "I think."

"You think? Or you hope?"

"Sometimes," said Jules, "I hardly know the difference."

A low hum permeated the tunnel, as if coming from some faraway machinery, and Jules noticed the pressure building inside his ears. This continued for several minutes, until he thought he couldn't take it anymore. Then he spied a faint light up ahead. He moved forward through the tunnel, until he reached its end, and stepped out into the forest.

114

PART TWO

CHAPTER 8

The Guardian of Tarsis

Jules emerged through the far side of the tunnel and onto the edge of a narrow, rocky dirt path, instantly engulfed by a sickly-sweet breeze that reminded him of overripe cantaloupes. He adjusted the old fedora against the harsh glare of the sun and glanced behind him. The back entrance to the underground passage was nothing but an indistinct jagged hole at the base of a white marble cliff, partially hidden by a large pear-shaped boulder coated with black lichen. The tunnel was so well camouflaged, in fact, that had Jules not known it was there, he would have walked right past it without so much as a second glance, thinking it was nothing but a shallow niche in the rock.

Jules took a deep breath, happy to be out of that stuffy place. He wasn't normally claustrophobic, but the tunnel had been creepy and had frightened him a little bit. At one point he had started to get dizzy and it had felt as if the entire world was rotating underneath his feet.

Bergen hopped off his shoulder and scampered into the sun, where he spread his arms and sucked in the rich-scented air, before flopping on his stomach and rolling in a patch of thick grass.

"There!" he said. "That'll get that awful smell out. I'll never get used to that passage." He sat up and looked at Jules, who was busy staring at his tiny friend. "Unlike their large cousins the cave trolls, woodland trolls do not particularly like to be in enclosed spaces, preferrin' the open expanse and soft ground of the forest."

"I'm not judging. I've just never seen a troll rolling around on the ground before."

"Hmph. Well, now that we're here, might as well search for somethin' to eat. Used to be a giant oak tree right over there, wide enough to be hollowed for a tea-room inside, but I suppose you've destroyed that."

"Next time I'll make sure there're plenty of carved-out oaks."

Bergen scrambled back to his feet and wandered around the edge of the clearing. As Jules watched his friend scour the forest floor for berries and small fruit, he assessed his surroundings.

Based on what Thisted and the others had told him, he expected the forest to be completely unrecognizable, like an alien landscape—full of mysterious plants and strange, unimaginable creatures that had sprouted up from the depths of his imagination. Thus Jules was disappointed to discover that everything appeared to be perfectly ordinary, at least so far as he could see. A thick tangle of elms, beeches, and pine trees pressed against the fringe of the path, huddled together as if holding a conference and whispering secrets between each other so he wouldn't hear them. A pair of squirrels hustled through the clearing and disappeared through thick brush. A thin layer of brown pine needles blanketed the ground, reminding him of autumn. Maybe the whole story of creating a new world by looking at a supposedly magic Map was nothing but a trick, a hoax. A scam.

But something wasn't right. It took Jules a moment to realize that, although he'd wandered the paths crisscrossing the woods behind the store countless times, everything seemed unfamiliar. This was confusing. He couldn't have been in that stuffy tunnel for more than five minutes, so surely he should be no more than a quarter-mile from home. Trying to get his bearings, he scrambled up the steep slope, hoping for a glimpse of his house. When he reached the top of the small rise, he saw nothing but trees in every direction, some with leaves of colors he'd never seen before.

"I guess they weren't lying after all." Then with a start he realized that the magic of the tunnel could have deposited them anywhere within this hidden world, perhaps even hundreds of miles away from where they had started, and that his ability to relocate this narrow crack in the cliff might well be his only chance of ever returning home. What if he couldn't find it again? He'd be wandering the forest forever, lost.

Then he had an idea. He fished around in his pants pockets until his fingers stumbled upon the canister of red lipstick he had discovered while exploring the Klepner house all those weeks ago, which he'd been carrying around all this time. Popping off the top, he scrawled a large 'X' on the enormous boulder, along with an arrow pointing toward the narrow cleft in the rock face. After this, he noticed there was still two good inches of lipstick left in the tube, so he replaced the top and dropped it back into his pocket.

"I wonder what those two gnomes packed for me," he thought aloud. "Might as well take a look while we're stopped." If it was one thing he'd learned from his time in the store, it was the importance of keeping track of inventory.

He slipped the tattered old backpack off his shoulders, unzipped it. It turned out that, in addition to the items they had mentioned when he was preparing to leave on his quest, Alesund and Algard had also loaded a length of rope, frayed at one end; a loaf of bread, with several slices partially eaten; a jar of peanut butter and a dull knife for spreading it; a half-dozen chocolate bars; a commemorative handheld telescope that his father once had bought for him at the county fair; and a large thermos, which was filled with apple cider that was strangely tart in not quite the right way. After all that, there was still enough room in the backpack for the large Map-book. Jules ran his fingers over the symbol on the cover of the white bird encircled by a trio of snakes before carefully slipping it back inside.

"Bergen!" he called. "Where have you gone off to? Time to go."

Almost immediately the troll appeared through a gap in a bush holding a handful of berries, his face smeared with purple jam.

"I'm comin', I'm comin'," Bergen said, suppressing a burp. "Jus' collectin' a little snack for later. You never know when berries will get scarce."

"Looks like you're not bothering to wait."

The troll burped softly. "Jus' makin' sure they're edible."

Together they set off. The path, littered with large stones and fallen branches, was nothing more than a deer trail, a few feet wide and lined with thorny bramble bushes. Jules dragged the bike alongside him, struggling to pull it over the rough terrain. But not far away he stumbled upon a wider, better-kept path, which was quite evidently the main forest road. One direction was blocked with fallen debris and some discarded construction barriers with flashing orange lights on top of them, which Jules took as a hint he was meant to go the other way. So without any further thought, Jules mounted the cherry-red bicycle and was soon wobbling along, trying to retain his balance.

"Have you ever ridden one of these contraptions before?" quizzed Bergen, eying Jules carefully. The troll was perched in the basket in the front of the bike, tightly grabbing the wire mesh in his tiny fists, but still banging his arms and shoulders whenever Jules veered sharply.

"I wouldn't say that exactly."

"What would you say then, if not 'yes' or 'no'?"

"Well . . . no, then, if you have to know. But I've seen other kids ride before, and it doesn't look too difficult. See? Already I'm getting the hang of it." As he addressed the troll, Jules momentarily took his eyes off the road, and he looked back just in time to notice some thick tree roots extending across the path.

"Hold on," he called, twisting the handlebars sharply. Yet he swerved too late, and the bike bounded over the obstacle, causing the front wheel to flare up and leave the ground. Bergen lost his hold on the basket, becoming temporarily airborne before landing hard.

"One would think," Bergen said, rubbing his bottom, "that a boy out on his very first bicycle ride would be more apt to watch where he was going."

"Sorry," Jules said, slowing. "It's just that I've never realized how much I'd like riding a bike, and I can't imagine a better day or place for it." He glanced around. "It's such a beautiful day. I wish we weren't in such a hurry to get to Pho Altis, and we could—"

"Watch out!" Bergen cried.

For while Jules had been distracted by the beauty of the forest, he neglected to notice the pile of rock and debris that blocked part of the road. This time there was no time to even attempt to avoid the obstruction. Jules shut his eyes and went right toward it.

The bicycle shuddered and Jules sensed the back wheel sliding out to the right as he passed over some wet leaves. He felt himself losing control. As he tried to remain upright, the bike veered off toward the edge of the road, toward a menacing-looking thicket. The bike vibrated sharply, and Jules's hands slipped off the handlebars in their entirety.

"Watch where yer going!" shouted Bergen, who was in a much more exposed position at the front of the bike, and more likely to take the brunt force of any accident. The troll gripped the basket, turning his knuckles white. "Left—no, right!"

Jules, of course, had no control over whether the bike went right *or* left, and was busy trying to grab hold of the handlebars again, but they weren't cooperating, as if they were excited to be on their own without a pair of hands guiding them. They turned this way and that way like a wild horse shaking its head when the rider drops the reins. But then at the very last moment before the bike ended up in the bushes, Jules was able to regain his balance and steer sharply back toward the center of the road. He hit the brakes just as Bergen lost his grip on the wires. The momentum flung the troll out of the basket and through the air, into a deep puddle left from a morning rainstorm.

"Sorry," Jules muttered with a shrug, as if this sort of thing was perfectly normal and should be expected.

Bergen sat up, wiped the mud from his face, and glared. "Maybe you should let me steer from now on."

"You'll have to grow a bit taller first."

Bergen scaled the tire and settled back into the basket. "Jus' try to keep us on the road, okay? And pay more attention in the future. Any attention at all will do."

"I promise," Jules agreed, stifling a chuckle.

Jules pedaled along through the woods with a new focus, intent on getting to Pho Altis without any further accidents. He continued forward until quite suddenly the road came to an end at a T-shaped intersection. He braked and rolled to a halt just in front of a large green sign with the words 'THE ROAD TO WISDOM BEGINS WITH SELF-AWARENESS' printed with purple ink that looked as if it had not yet completely dried.

"Now that doesn't help one bit," Jules complained, after working through the longer words. "I wonder which way we are supposed to go next." He dismounted his bicycle and peered down the new road in both directions, neither of which looked particularly inviting.

"One way is as good as the other, unless it isn't," a gravelly voice said from nearby.

Jules looked up. Perched atop the sign was the largest bird he had ever seen. It had a long, curved beak, and was covered with mottled feathers. One of the bird's black eyes was closed, but with its other eye it glared at him and the bicycle. Jules had never heard of a talking bird before, but under the circumstances he thought it best to be polite, and besides, perhaps the creature could provide some useful assistance.

"Hello there," he said in his most friendly voice. "Do you happen to know the right way to go?"

"There's only one right way," the bird responded. "Although there's a left way also. Of course," it added with a shrill squawk, "if you were facing the way you came, the right way would be the left way, and the left way would be the right way, and we'd be all mixed up."

"I think I'm already mixed up," Jules answered. "Who are you?"

"I am the Guardian of Tarsis," the bird said, fluffing up its feathers so that it looked twice its actual size. "But you can call me Max." The bird flew down and teetered on the handlebars, ringing the silver bell several times with its crooked beak. "I do so love the sound of bells," continued the bird. "They remind me of dinnertime. Don't you think so?"

"Why—I've never really thought about it," Jules answered. "You see—"

"I don't suppose you'd mind if I sat here for a little bit," Max continued, not paying any attention to what Jules had started to say. "The view from atop the sign gets quite dull. The same scenery, day after day. Besides, I've never ridden on a bicycle before, and it looks like such terrific fun." The bird squawked loudly. "Which way are you headed?"

"That's just it," Jules said, glad to finally get a word in. "I don't know, and I'm afraid we could be lost."

Max ruffled his feathers, an action that sounded like someone shuffling a pack of playing cards. "If you don't know where you're going, either way will get you there just as well as the other."

"But I do know. We're trying to get to Pho Altis."

"Then why did you just say you didn't know?"

"It's not so much the place as it is the location, if you follow me. Could you help us with directions?"

"It's quite simple, really," Max said, grooming one of his wings where the feathers hadn't quite settled back to where they belonged. "You just have to continue along the road, along the road, along the road. Can't miss it."

"But—that doesn't help at all," said Jules, trying to keep his temper in check. "Which direction are we to go in?"

Max squawked noisily and coughed up a small bone before responding. "What does it matter? One way is just as good as another. Only the landscape differs."

"Not to us," Jules said. "We're somewhat in a hurry. You see—"

"Let me try," Bergen croaked from inside the basket. "Which is the *shortest* way to Pho Altis?"

"Oh, what a pretty pet mouse you have," said Max, who now noticed Bergen for the first time. "And polite, too."

"I'm not a mouse, you stupid, mangy bird. I'm a troll, a woodland troll at that."

"Mouse or troll, it doesn't matter," Max replied, ringing the bell three more times in succession. "Especially as the mealtime bell just rang." With another shrill call, the bird reached inside the wire basket, snapping its beak open and shut several times as if cutting string with a pair of scissors. Before Bergen could get out of range, Max caught hold of his tunic just above the waistline and snipped a small hole in it. As Bergen glared at the bird and shook his fists in anger, Max peered at Bergen with a nasty grin, snapping his beak in a Spanish rhythm.

"That ain't fair," Bergen complained. "It ain't mealtime at all. You rang that bell yerself."

"So?"

"So, yer nothin' but a cheat and a scoundrel, Bird." Sensing his opportunity, Bergen lunged forward and yanked out a few of the bird's breast feathers, and stuck the ends in Max's eyes. Max shrieked.

Before Max could renew the assault, Jules lifted the bird by its carefully-manicured talons and placed it out of reach of the basket. "Can't you tell us anything helpful?" he asked.

Max puffed up his feathers and shut one eye. "The shortest distance between two points is often a straight line, unless you are travelling along a curved surface, in which case you will need to use higher mathematics to perform the relevant calculations."

"This is a waste of time," Bergen said. "We're not going to learn anything useful from this creature. You might as well take out the Map and figure things out for yerself."

"But Thisted said—"

"I'm sure it's okay," Bergen answered. "We're in the middle of nowhere, and there's no one here but this stupid crow. I don't think there's any danger."

"Oooh, yes, the Map, the Map!" cackled the bird. "Map Map Map Map *Map*."

"Oh, hush up," Jules said. "And give us some privacy already." He nudged the bird with his hands, until Max lost his balance and flew back to the top of the sign.

Jules flipped down the kickstand and dismounted the bicycle, leaving it tilting on the bumpy road. He lifted the large book from his backpack and ran his finger along the edge, searching for the ribbon bookmark, which wasn't at all easy to do, since he was keeping his eyes trained on Max to make sure the large bird wasn't intent on causing trouble.

"Gosh darn it," Jules said. "I can hardly do one thing at a time, let alone two." For just a moment, he looked down at the Map, trying to locate the correct page.

But a moment was all Max needed. Before Jules realized what was happening, the bird swooped back down off the sign, wrenched the book from Jules's grasp, and flew off along the road with the Map of Eternity clenched in its claws.

"It was just a trick!" Jules exclaimed, cursing at himself for his inattentiveness.

"After that bird!" cried Bergen.

Jules jumped back on the bicycle and began pedaling furiously. As he pumped his legs, the bike sped down the road, throwing up gravel in its wake. Jules felt his breath starting to waver, but didn't dare stop or slow down. He sucked in lungful after lungful of air, trying to ignore his cramping thighs, as he stayed in pursuit of the large black bird.

"Faster! Faster!" Bergen encouraged from his station in the front of the wire basket. "I think we're gaining!"

Soon they had pulled to within just a few feet of Max. Jules reached up with one hand, keeping his other tight around the handlebar grip. Closer and closer he came to the bird, until his fingers hovered just inches away from the ends of its tail feathers. He lunged, squeezed.

"Gotcha!" he shouted, as he closed his hands around Max's tail.

And missed. For at that moment the road dipped, and Jules found himself zooming down a steep hill, completely out of control.

Now catching Max had taken on secondary importance. Jules grasped the handlebars, trying to keep his balance. But as the bike reached the bottom of the dip, the front wheel hit a small lip of dirt and crud, the bike tipped forward, and Jules was hurtled over the top of the handlebars into the thick grass on the side of the road. The bike collapsed in the middle of the road in a tangled mess, and Max flew to a nearby rooftop and began cackling with laughter.

Jules sat on the ground in a heap. He had a scrape on his knee, and there was a dull pain in his shoulder, but otherwise he had come out of it unscathed.

"Bergen?" he called. "Are you all right?"

The troll crawled out from under the twisted frame and stretched his muscles. "Are you kiddin' me? That was awesome! Let's do it again!"

Jules cast a glance at the wreckage. "I don't think we're going to be doing that again soon, or any other riding, for that matter. But the important thing is to first get the Map back from that stupid bird." He looked up at Max, who was paying no attention to them and was once again preening his breast feathers. "Any ideas?"

"Leave this to me." Bergen cleared his throat and began to taunt Max with a string of crude insults, but Max didn't budge from his perch.

"I think we need a plan that appeals to his baser instincts," Jules said, rummaging through his backpack. "Aha—here we go!" He whooped and clapped his hands three or four times until Max looked down to see what all the fuss was about. "It's snack time!" Jules yelled, snapping apart one of the chocolate bars and tossing a small chunk up toward the rooftop.

As he had hoped, Max reached out with his claw to pluck the piece of chocolate from midair, dropping the Map-book in the process. As the bird ate, the Map slid down the rows of clay roof tiles and fell neatly onto the ground, where Jules picked it up with a great sigh of relief.

"All's well that end's well," said Jules, hugging the book between his arms and promising himself to be more careful in the future.

"Yes," Bergen said with a sigh, "but not for the bicycle."

Jules walked into the street. The red bicycle was curled up in the dirt like an injured animal. The tires hadn't popped, but part of the frame was bent, and the handlebars were facing the wrong direction. Yet it was nothing that couldn't be fixed with the proper equipment. Finding the right tools in the middle of the forest was another matter, though.

But they weren't in the forest, at least not anymore; the chase had taken them someplace completely different. "It looks like we're in some sort of town," said Jules, glancing around. "Maybe we could find someone here who could help us." It was then that he noticed the state everything was in. The buildings leaned at odd angles and were nearly falling apart, while the road itself was dusted with rubble and pockmarked with deep craters.

"Welcome to Tarsis," Max said, no longer cackling.

CHAPTER 9

Tarsis

Jules ambled down the partially destroyed cobblestone street. "What happened here, Max?" he called out. "Where is everyone? The town seems to be deserted."

"I don't know," Max replied, squawking twice. The large crow had fluttered along behind Jules, and was now perched on the edge of a nearby rooftop, probably in the hope Jules would toss him another piece of chocolate.

"I thought you were the Guardian of Tarsis."

"Truth be told," Max said, "I've never been here before."

"Then what is it you do, exactly?" Jules asked in a suspicious tone.

Max looked away, unable to meet Jules's eyes. "I really just direct traffic at the intersection."

"Harass passersby, you mean," countered Bergen, who had yet to forgive Max for his earlier behavior.

"I just wanted to be a Guardian," Max said, sniffing. "I sent the application, signed and notarized, of course, along with the necessary filing fee. All I got back was a form letter telling me that Tarsis didn't need a Guardian at this time, but that there was a position open as a carrion feeder. A carrion feeder! *Squawk.* Why, any self-loathing vulture could do that."

Max looked so forlorn that Jules let the bird land on his outstretched hand, and scratched a particularly hard-to-reach spot in the center of his back until Max seemed to perk up.

"It's okay, Max," Jules said, trying to cheer the creature up. "I'm sure you'd make a terrific Guardian if you were ever given a chance."

"BUT NOW IT'S TOO LATE," the bird wailed loudly. "THERE'S NO ONE LEFT AT ALL."

"Thanks to you," Bergen muttered under his breath, as Max collapsed in a flood of tears and sobs.

"Oh, leave him alone, Bergen. I think the poor thing is upset enough as it is."

Max nodded between sniffles and blew a raspberry at the troll when he thought Jules wasn't watching.

"I have an idea, Max," Jules said. "You can be *my* Guardian. You know, look out for me and stuff."

Max brightened. "You really mean it?" he asked. "You'd really do that for me?"

"It wouldn't be quite the same as being the Guardian for an entire town, but I'm sure you'll do a great job. What do you say?"

Max visibly weighed his choices for a moment before seeming to come to a decision. He cleared his throat with a squawk. "Being your Guardian will *hardly* tax my extensive abilities in the field," he said before hastily adding, "but I'm just looking for a start in the business. A claw in the door. After all, you have to start somewhere, and you never know where an opportunity will lead."

"My Mom is always telling me the same thing. So what do you think?"

"I accept," said Max, fluffing up his feathers.

"I can't believe you're doing this," Bergen grumbled. "This bird is nothing but trouble, mark my words."

"Hush, Bergen. Max, why don't you start by trying to figure out what happened to everyone who used to live here? Maybe there's still someone left who can help us."

"Will do, boss!" Max saluted and zigzagged off through the air, disappearing over a line of orange roofs, squawking as he flew.

"Well, Bergen," Jules said once the bird had gone, "let's look around. Maybe we'll find some tools in one of these buildings so we can fix the bike ourselves and be on our way.

After all, we've still got a long way to go before we reach Pho Altis."

Jules and Bergen wandered through the streets, peeking through the clouded windows of some of the buildings, until by chance they stumbled upon a hardware store with a selection of tools still inside. The place was empty, but after scouring the shelves Jules was able to locate a rubber hammer and a matching wrench from the same set.

"I think this should do the trick," Jules said, slipping them into his backpack. "Come on, let's go." On the way out, he pulled out a gold coin and left it on the countertop.

"Why'd you do that?" Bergen asked.

"Oh, just in case the owner returns. My mother told me it isn't right to take things without paying for them, no matter where I am."

"I think you're overpaying a bit."

"It's okay." Jules glanced around at the mess. "Besides, it looks like they can use the extra money."

"If they ever come back."

"Yeah," Jules agreed. "If they ever come back."

They reversed their steps until they reached the bicycle, which wasn't at all where Jules thought he had left it. He untwisted the frame until the bike was spread out flat along the cobblestones, and proceeded to work on the fender with the rubber hammer. He banged away as carefully as he could, smoothing the dents to the rhythm of *Skip to my Lou*. It was slow going, but soon he had gotten the trick of it, and gradually the fender was pounded more or less into the right shape. Once he had completed that task, he turned his attention to the handlebars. This was more difficult, but eventually he was able to loosen the large metal nut and straighten them out. After he retightened the nut, Jules mounted the bike and tried riding it down the street.

"As good as new," Jules said upon his return, and while that wasn't quite true—the fender was dented horribly from the hammer, and the beautiful red paint had scraped off in places—the bike was at least in working order once again. "Come on, Bergen," he said, flipping down the kickstand. "Let's get out of here before Max returns."

"What about all that 'you can be my guardian' mumbo-jumbo?"

"I was just trying to make him feel better. Really."

"So you don't trust him, either?"

"Should I? He already took the Map from me once. I think he's just out to cause mischief and cares only about himself. The sooner we're free of him, the better."

"Don't forget that he tried to bite my head off."

Jules stroked Bergen's hair. "That didn't endear him to me, either. But while we have a few minutes of privacy, perhaps we should take a good look at the Map and figure out where we are and how to get where we want to go. In case he follows us when we leave."

Jules sat down in the shade and slipped the Map-book from his knapsack, marveling about how heavy it felt in his hands. In his backpack, it seemed to hardly weigh a thing.

After placing it on the ground, he swung open the cover to the page marked by the ribbon bookmark and watched the colors swirl in the air above the pages until they formed shapes, and the shapes connected into recognizable features and landmarks. The map looked much different here in the outdoors than it did in the dark of the Klepner basement, even while sitting in the shade. The indirect sunlight produced a yellow glow and caused the image to shimmer like the air above hot summer pavement, making Jules lightheaded and a little dizzy. He blinked hard, trying to concentrate, until he learned to relax his eyes and let the details come to him in their own time.

"It really is pretty," Jules said as his eyes lingered on the snow-capped mountain range that sliced through the center of the hologram. "It's too bad it won't last forever. Bergen, how long will it take before all of this starts to deteriorate? Do you know?"

The troll shrugged. "Sixty or seventy years, probably. Sometimes longer, sometimes less. It really depends."

"Oh? Depends on what?"

"On you, of course, silly."

"Huh? What do you mean?"

"Don't you know? You an' the Map are bonded to each other now. This world will continue to exist for as long as you're alive."

"So the person who created the previous world—"

"He died."

"Oh." There was an uncomfortable pause.

"It always takes a few years for the old world to completely fade away after the Reformer dies," Bergen explained. "Like old memories."

"Whoever he was, he must've been pretty special," Jules said. "Do you know what ever happened to the princess he rescued from the count? The Copper Princess?"

"No one knows. She vanished and no one ever saw her again." Bergen popped a coffee bean into his mouth and chewed. "It doesn't matter anymore. If she was still alive somewhere, she would've vanished along wi' everythin' else when you looked at the Map. Just ancient history now that no one'll ever remember."

"That's too bad. I think I would've liked to meet her." Jules looked down at the Map. "Hey, I think I found where we are." Jules pointed toward the image of a small town nestled in a sea of rolling hills. "Do you see the red dot?"

Bergen nodded. "It looks like there's somethin' written there, too."

Jules squinted hard. "I think you're right. Your eyesight is better than mine." He leaned forward until his nose was just inches away from the hologram and read the tiny block letters. "T-A-R-S-I-S. *Tarsis.* Well, that clinches it. That's where we are, no mistaking it, and Max was telling the truth."

"Harrumph. I still don't trust that mangy bird."

"Forget about him, will you? He's gone."

"So now we know where we are," Bergen said, "but we still need to know where we're going. How do we get to Pho Altis from here?"

"Pho Altis, the Fortress of Everlasting Light. It sounds so strange when you say it out loud. I guess the first step is to find it on the Map." Jules scanned the holographic image, even circling it several times without success. "Oh, dear," he said at last as his frustration hit the boiling point. "I do wish this thing had an index."

Just like that a register of places appeared midair, glowing neon blue. "Well, that's certainly helpful," Jules said. "I wish someone had mentioned it before." He scrolled through the alphabetical list until he reached the entry for Pho Altis. He touched it with his finger, and instantaneously a small but bright green light lit up and began to flash at even intervals.

"That must be it," he said, pointing. "Why, compared to where we are going, we've hardly gotten very far at all." He traced the distance with his finger. "You know, from this viewpoint, the White Fortress hardly looks very sinister, don't you think?"

"Don't be fooled. I can only imagine what sort of things are goin' on there right now."

"Do you think if I tried hard enough I could see my mother inside?" Without waiting for an answer, Jules waved his hands in a circular motion, and the portion of the Map containing Pho Altis expanded as if in a bubble until reaching maximum magnification. He brought his head as close as he could to the Fortress, shifting his feet to get the best angle. "The windows are dark."

"Let me look." Bergen hopped forward to get a better view. "There seem to be a lot of creatures assembling outside. It looks like the count is starting to amass his forces."

"You can really see all that?"

"Of course. Haven't you ever heard the expression, 'He has eyes like a hawk'?"

"Yeah, sure, but what does that—"

"You ever wonder what hawks say to each other?"

"Uh . . . can't say that I have."

"They say, 'That hawk can see like a troll.' An' that's the truth."

Jules looked at his friend skeptically and asked, "Do you see anything else?"

"Well, if you'd been payin' better attention, you'd have seen the moat of vapor fire surroundin' the Fortress, and the front gate carved from skulls and bone. Don't need a troll's vision to see *that*."

"Oh." Jules bit his lower lip in thought. "We'll have to worry about that later. For now, let's just focus on getting there." He traced the route with his finger. "The hard parts are going to be crossing those mountains and getting across all this water." He pointed to the large blue area near the center of the Map, which was conveniently labeled 'Crystal Sea' in block letters. "It's too big to go around without losing too much time. We'll have to find some way to cross it. Hopefully we'll be able to hitch a ride on a boat. Then it shouldn't be much farther until we're there." He ran his finger along the entire route once more, forward and backward, until he thought he had it memorized.

"That's odd," he added. "It looks like there's a dark smudge on the Map. Do you see? It's not far, just over that hill in the middle of the forest. It's almost as if there's a blank spot." He rubbed his hands together. "Do you think the world is deteriorating again?"

"That's impossible," Bergen said. "You're still alive, aren't you? It's probably just a low-lying cloud or some smoke. You better put that thing away, anyway," he whispered. "I think there's someone over there who's been watching us this whole time."

Jules turned and looked at the buildings across the street, and caught a brief glimpse of a face before it quickly withdrew from a window. "I think you're right. Come on. Let's see if we can finally get some answers."

He stood up and began to cross the street. But before he got to the other side, a door opened and a small figure popped out, one that Jules was shocked to recognize.

"Betsy Bottomsley!"

"Hi, Jules," Betsy said. She was wearing a blue sun dress with white trim along the hem and on the edges of the sleeves, and looked at him shyly. As usual, around her neck hung a large clove of garlic.

"What are you *doing* here, Betsy?"

"I got angry when my parents didn't believe me when I told them I saw a little man in your store," she explained. "So I ran away." She waved at Bergen, who was lounging on Jules's foot. "Hi, little man."

Bergen stood and bowed. "Hello, Betsy. Bergen the Woodland Troll, at yer service. Glad t' meetcha an' all of that."

"I'm glad to meet you, too," Betsy said, performing a neat curtsy.

"But how did you *get* here?" Jules asked. "We're miles and miles from home. You couldn't have walked here all by yourself."

She shrugged. "I don't know. I just entered the woods and I ended up here somehow."

"Listen, Betsy," Jules said. "You can't stay here, okay? I can't look after you. You have to go home."

"Well, I'm not going home. I'm tired of the way my parents always treat me. You wouldn't understand what it's like. You live such a great life, in that neat store of yours. They make me wear this dumb piece of garlic around my neck all the time. I can't stand it. All the other kids laugh at me."

"Why do your parents make you wear that thing, anyway?" Jules asked. "It stinks. Is it to keep from getting sick? Or to ward off vampires? My dad once told me that was just a myth."

"I don't know. And you know what? I'm not going to do it anymore." She grabbed hold of the garlic bulb and yanked hard until the string broke, leaving it dangling from her hand. "There!"

"If you're not gonna be needin' that . . ." Bergen said, his voice trailing off.

"Oh! Why, of course you may have it." Betsy snapped off two cloves and handed them to Bergen, who began to nibble away.

"Well, I don't know what I'm going to do with you," Jules said. "You can't remain here in this town all by yourself, and you can't come with me. It's too dangerous."

"Why? Where are you going?"

"I'm going to rescue my mom. She was kidnapped by a man named Count Barchmod, and is being held prisoner in the White Fortress of Pho Altis, which is across the other side of the forest and really far away."

Betsy sighed. "You live such an exciting life. So why can't I come with you?"

"You're too young, Betsy."

"I am not!"

"Yes, you are. You'll just get lost or hurt or worse. Besides, I'm going to get there on my bike, and you won't be able to keep up."

Betsy opened her mouth to protest, but she was drowned out by a distinct buzzing sound that seemed to be coming from all around them.

"What's that noise?" Jules shouted, struggling to be heard over the din.

"We'd better hide," Betsy yelled. "They're coming back."

That was more than enough for Bergen to hear. He zipped off through the street without looking back and disappeared behind some debris piled in the gutter.

"What's coming back?" asked Jules, who lacked Bergen's instinct for self-preservation.

His question was unnecessary, however, for at that moment a swarm of insects descended upon the town. But these were unlike any insects Jules had ever seen before. They had bodies the size of peaches and two sets of silvery wings that were nearly a half-foot long. The swarm engulfed the town like a hurricane. They tore tiles from the roofs and drilled holes in the streets with their stingers, which protruded down from their midsections and vibrated like jackhammers. Jules was instantly reminded of piranhas that lived in the Amazon River and were said to eat anything alive. In class Jules had once seen a film of a school of these fish devouring a cow in a matter of minutes. So, too, was the speed at which these insects attacked. It was a feeding frenzy, and the town was the food. Now Jules understood why all the buildings appeared to be falling apart, and why no one lived in Tarsis anymore.

"Come on," Betsy begged, tugging on Jules's sleeve. "We have to get inside before it's too late."

But it was too late. The horde of insects noticed the two children standing in the cobblestone street and stopped causing mischief. They flew together to form a giant sphere, a swirling, churning mass of beating wings so tightly packed that it was impossible to distinguish among them. To Jules they looked like a cloud of black smoke as they swarmed round and round, faster and faster. Then, just like that, the swarm lowered itself to the ground. Jules watched as the thousands of insects transformed into the shape of a naked human body, a woman of such beauty that Jules couldn't look away. Unashamed, the woman towered over Jules, hair flowing over her body in waves.

In a beautiful voice, it—or them—or she—spoke to him. "I know who you are," it said. A low-level hum buzzed between words. "You carry the Map of Eternity with you."

Jules nodded, unable to answer.

The woman shut her eyes and inhaled deeply, as if she was learning everything about him just by his scent. She held out her hands, and several of the insects flew off from her arms and circled Jules's head, before returning to rejoin the rest of the swarm.

She opened her eyes. "Your name is Jules."

He nodded again, tried to move, but his legs were frozen in place.

"Do not be afraid, Jules," she said. "I am not here to hurt you. I have come for the Map, and then you may go, unharmed." The woman floated toward him, still holding out her hands.

It's not a person, he told himself over and over. *It's something bad.* "Who—who are you?" he stammered, finally finding his voice.

"I am Alexis. I am forever. The Map is for me, not you, and it is time for you to give it to me." Alexis's arms turned into wisps of black smoke, and extended farther toward Jules, until they nearly touched him.

Jules struggled, but was still held in place by her beauty, mesmerized. As if controlled by a puppeteer, he slowly reached into his backpack and removed the Map-book, and held it out toward Alexis.

Alexis smiled, an impossibly beautiful smile that made Jules feel warm all over. Her hands broke off into their component insects, which flew over to the Map and began to eat away at the leather cover. "Mmm," Alexis moaned. "I can feel its power inside me, energizing me."

Then Jules felt a sharp pain in his forearm. "Ow!" he cried, retracting his arm. Startled by his sudden movement, the insects flew from the Map-book, which now sported several holes across the cover. They rejoined Alexis and merged back into parts of her body and head. Jules looked down. Betsy had pinched him, and hard.

"Come *on*," she said, grabbing Jules by the hand. "She's just trying to trick you."

Betsy had broken the spell. Jules looked once again at the woman, and saw that she was gone, and in her place swarmed the mass of insects.

"Give it to me!" cried Alexis, now morphed into the likeness of the librarian. "Give me the Map, Jules, or you'll get chocolate on the pages! You cannot take it out without your own library card!"

"It's reaching into your mind," Betsy said. "She's done it to me, too. It's not really that librarian lady. You have to resist."

Now Alexis took the form of Ms. Binkley, and begun to chant "Your report must be twenty pages long and not a single page less, we wouldn't want a repeat of last year's fiasco," over and OVER and OVER and Jules tried to cover his ears with his hands, but it did no good, for Alexis's voice was inside his head now. Still chanting, she crept closer and closer, until she was just inches away . . .

And then Betsy pinched Jules on the arm a second time.

That did it. Again aware of what was happening around him, Jules hugged the Map close to his body and backed away. Once more Alexis morphed into a swirling ball of insects. The swarm zoomed high into the air, reformed into the body of the beautiful woman, and then flew at Jules in attack. Her mouth opened impossibly wide, revealing the black depth of the horror within. There was nothing Jules and Betsy could do, for there was no way to outrun this foul menace. They stood there, hand in hand, awaiting the end. The insects reached out to Jules and Betsy, to envelop them and tear away their flesh—

—and were hit by something midair, and knocked back. It was Max, the self-proclaimed Guardian of Tarsis, now appointed the Guardian of Jules. Then Jules saw that Max was more than just a large crow, he was a supernatural spirit himself, a demon to those who dared stand against him. Max darted through the sky until his black wings were nothing but distorted shadows, patches of darkness outlined by an incandescent blue light, a Whirling Dervish of the air. Max had grown to three times his original size, his beak now the length of hedge clippers and as sharp as razor wire. And in this ancient form Max fought the swarm of insects, snapping at them and swallowing them whole. The insects fought back against this new threat, surrounding Max, trying to bite at him, but Max would not be deterred.

"Run, Jules," Max squawked. "Run, and don't look back."

Jules whirled and ran down the street with his backpack flopping on his shoulder by one strap, pulling Betsy behind him by the hand. When they reached the bicycle, Bergen was already waiting for them, perched in the wire basket and urging them forward. Jules mounted the bike and took off down the street, with Betsy holding on for dear life.

CHAPTER 10

The Valley

Jules sped down the road, gasping for air and with a scream stuck halfway down his throat. He heard the terrible sounds of the battle between Max and the swarm of giant insects taking place in the air behind him. But Jules heeded Max's words and did not stop, nor did he look back. He strained at the pedals, pumping his legs until the trees and bushes melted into streaks of green.

Bergen stood in the basket at the front of the bike, grasping the metal wires in his gnarled fists, while Betsy sat behind Jules, crammed onto the very end of the narrow bicycle seat. She held Jules tightly around his waist, trying not to fall off. The bike bounced over an uneven patch in the road, and Jules's backpack sprang up and hit her square in the nose. She sneezed into his hair, but didn't let go.

The road narrowed, and the forest closed in around them. By now they were miles and miles from Tarsis, and could no longer hear the sounds of the air battle. Jules wondered what was happening and hoped that Max was going to be okay.

"Well, Betsy," he said, "I guess we're stuck with you now."

"Good," she said. "I like both of you a lot better than that bug lady."

They rode on, stopping only to eat and sleep. Betsy told Jules about her family, about how her parents would never let her do anything fun for fear that she would get hurt. For his part, Jules told her about his mother and father, and about the amazing Map that he carried with him on his quest. Before long it seemed to both of them that they had known each other forever, and they soon discovered they had more in common than being the target of the other kids' taunts and mean-spirited teasing. As they rode along, they discussed everything from their classmates to places they liked to go after school when they wanted to be alone. For Jules, who was used to being quiet among others, this was quite a change, and he found he was nearly bubbling over with things he wanted to tell her. Betsy was a good listener, and when she smiled back and laughed at the right places, Jules felt warm and tingly all over.

Then they came to a place that caused the hairs on the back of Jules's neck to stand on end. He slammed on the brakes and stared. Up ahead, darkness covered the land and nothing grew. All the foliage was gone, replaced by black rock and sand like a giant lava field. Everything was shrouded in shadow, as if a great storm cloud had covered the sky, yet the sun was shining from up above. It was as if he was looking at pure nothingness. "What is this place?" Jules asked.

"This must be the blank spot you saw on the Map back in Tarsis," said Bergen, scratching his stomach absentmindedly.

"There's nothing here," Jules said. "Nothing at all." Steeling his nerves, he dismounted the bicycle and walked over to the very edge of the dark spot. He stood there, straining his eyes as he peered into the void, trying to make out more detail. The lack of anything to focus on made him feel lightheaded, as if he was balanced on the tip of a pin in the center of the universe where the wrong movement in any direction would cause him to tumble endlessly through the emptiness of space. He felt strength and confidence seep from his essence, leaving only a hollow shell through which only his breath flowed. But as he turned his head and saw the trees behind him, the empty feeling immediately vanished.

"Be careful, Jules!" Betsy warned. "It might be dangerous!"

Jules nodded, and then before he could stop himself, he reached down and touched the blackened earth with his bare hand.

He heard Betsy gasp behind him. "Jules!" she cried. "Why did you do that? Are you okay?"

"Yeah, I think so," he replied. He wiggled his fingers. "See? No damage." Then, still unable to resist, he reached down again and rubbed his fingers along the smooth rock. "It's as if this part was skipped entirely when the world was Reformed."

Bergen frowned. "I've never heard of anythin' ever happenin' like this before," he said. "When we get back, we should tell Thisted and the others about it. Maybe they have an explanation."

"This is what I picture the moon to look like," Jules said. "Lifeless, and dark, and cold. What do you think, Betsy?"

"It gives me the willies," Betsy said, shivering. "Can we get out of here, please, before anything bad happens to us?"

"Okay, Betsy. I'm coming." But Jules didn't turn. Instead, as if pulled forward by a giant magnet, he took several steps forward.

"No!" Bergen shouted, but it was too late. Jules stepped into the black void.

Now that he was completely inside the dark spot, Jules was able to discern the contours of land stretching out in front of him. The rocks and sand were no longer black; they appeared to Jules as different shades of gray, interspersed with fluorescent blue flakes. Jules saw an energy field pass over his hands and face, white and ghost-like, like wisps of fog on a cool spring morning. He felt the hair on his head rise and stand out in all directions.

Jules turned to look at Betsy and Bergen, but they were gone. All he could see in that direction was a bright halo of light stretched along the edge of the void. He turned back and took another step deeper into the abyss, and a feeling of dizziness washed through him. He had tried to walk forward but could have sworn he had traveled sideways. He tried again and the same thing happened.

He heard a faint scuttling sound from near his feet. He looked down at the rock and noticed a pair of crabs, their shells a swirl of fluorescent blue and yellow. Something about the crabs struck him as odd, though, and it took him a moment to recognize what it was. The crabs were walking in a straight line, not sideways as he was used to seeing. Jules took another step forward and ended up one stride to his right.

"I'd better get out of here," he said. His voice echoed back toward him, over and over, indecipherable and unrecognizable. Jules fell to his hands and knees, and he tried to crawl back the way he had come. The dizzy feeling returned. He shut his eyes, but the dizziness didn't go away. He kept advancing, not even sure he was traveling in a straight line, when he felt something grab his jacket and drag him across the ground. A sharp sense of endangerment surged through him. He squealed, swiping at his body trying to get the thing off of him, away from him.

All movement stopped. Jules opened his eyes. Betsy stood over him, looking down into his face with concern. Bergen was on the ground near his head, slapping him in the cheek.

"Jules! Jules!" Betsy shouted. "Can you hear me?"

"Of course I can hear you. I'm not deaf. What happened?"

"We saw you came back to the edge of the dark spot, and then start crawling in circles," she said. "But you were close enough for me to pull you out."

Jules sat up. "Thanks, Betsy."

"What was in there?" she asked. "What did you see?"

But he just shook his head and refused to answer, partly because he didn't want to frighten her, and partly because he was still trying to understand it himself. "I think we better go around," was all he would say.

The black spot was so large across it took them nearly an hour to travel past it. As he pedaled, Jules was careful to keep his distance from the edge, so he wouldn't be affected by that strange magnetic pull again and be tempted to steer the bike inside. Once on the other side, they soon located the road, and continued along their way with Jules still refusing to discuss what he had experienced.

The road twisted through a copse of silver-barked trees leading downward into a great valley. Jules felt the wind whip through his hair as he coasted down the long hill. As he rode, Bergen belted out some old favorites from the front of the bike in his gravelly voice. One was called *My Old Troll was a Very Ugly Soul;* another was *There Was a Troll Maiden that Swallowed a Fly.*

The valley was shady and cool, a rift in the earth between steep green hillocks on both sides. Waterfalls streamed from the slopes, tumbling down rocks and meandering through the trees.

A whooshing noise filled the air, reminding Jules of the sound Ms. Binkley would make when trying to get the class to quiet down during assemblies, although softer, not as frantic.

Large birds with long, colorful tail feathers called down from the branches. At times in the distance came a louder cry, an elephant-like bellow from some large beast that remained hidden.

Jules rode along with Betsy behind him, laughing at each other's jokes and trying to out-do each other with their storytelling. "This is the most fun I've ever had," Betsy admitted.

"Really?"

"My parents never let me go out by myself and simply ride around on my bike, and they certainly don't like it when I tell stories. 'You have to live in the here and now,'" she imitated in a low masculine-sounding voice, before erupting in a flurry of laughter. "I'm glad we're friends."

"I don't think anyone's ever said that to me before. Usually they just nod their head when I talk, then make an excuse to leave as soon as possible. In fact, I don't think I've ever had a friend at all, at least someone who would admit to it."

Bergen coughed loudly.

"I mean, a human friend," Jules added with a smile.

"But you tell the best stories," Betsy said. "You really don't share them with anyone?"

"My father told the best stories. I just try to remember and repeat them the best I can. The bad parts are where I've completely forgotten and have to fill the gaps myself."

"You really miss him, don't you?"

"I do. Everything changed when he died. I feel like I lost both him and my mom too, if that makes sense."

"My grandmother died when I was little. I don't remember her very well. I have a photo of me sitting on her lap and twisting her nose. She was smiling, so it couldn't have hurt very much."

"Or maybe it did hurt, but it was worth it to have you with her."

"I guess."

"Do you like your parents?"

Betsy paused. "I'm not sure. Sometimes when I'm around them I feel like I can't just be myself. Sometimes I just want to be silly and laugh at things that seem odd, like how some trees look like they are trying to stand up straight and others like they fell asleep on their feet. Sometimes I feel too embarrassed to tell them things like that. I wish I had a brother or sister to share things with."

"Me, too, Betsy. Me, too. I guess a friend can be just as good."

A few evenings later, after they had ridden for several days, they stopped for the night near a spring that bubbled up from a rift in the earth, feeding a stream that snaked across the plain. A low-hanging fog hugged the ground like a silver blanket. While Bergen wandered off, Jules noticed some odd-looking beans on a nearby bush. He pulled some off and nibbled.

"Wow," he said. "These are amazing. I've never had beans that tasted like this." He offered some to Betsy.

"These *are* good," she agreed. "Much better than most of the stuff my parents bring home from your store. No offense."

Jules shrugged. "What, you don't like lima beans?"

Betsy giggled. "I hide them under my fork."

"I do that also," Jules admitted. "Sometimes I pretend to scratch my leg, and I slip a handful into the top of my sock."

"Ewww." Betsy wrinkled her nose. "But these are really, really good, and I could eat them all day. Maybe we should take some for later."

Jules nodded. "That's not a bad idea. I'll bet I can use them to make a bean stew."

As Jules pulled more of the beans from the bush and stuffed them into his backpack, Bergen returned carrying a pair of golden fish he had caught upstream. It was a welcome break from the steady diet of peanut butter sandwiches and energy bars. Jules built a fire using some of the remaining matches from the Klepner house. Recalling how his father had done it once when they had gone camping, he made a little clearing, sweeping away the dead leaves with his shoe, and carefully placed a ring of stones around the fire pit for safety. Then he built a small tower, with larger, thicker branches on the bottom and thin twigs laid across the top for easy kindling. He went through eight or ten matches before the fire finally caught. Jules looked at the flames licking the edges of the pit proudly and did a little dance with joy. If his classmates could see him now!

"Stop celebratin' and start roastin," complained Bergen, whose arms were too short to do the cooking himself.

So Jules roasted the fish, using sturdy branches as wooden spits. As they ate, Jules studied the mountains that loomed ominously before them. Over the past few days he had watched the mountains grow closer and closer, and finally they had nearly reached the edge of the first few foothills, which overlooked the far end of the valley like sentries on watch. He looked up at the ring of snow and ice capping the highest peaks and wondered how they'd get over the summit and what they'd find up there. Would there be mountain lions or bears, or even white-furred snow giants that would hurl boulders down at them as they climbed upwards? Well, starting tomorrow, they'd find out. He thought again of his mother, of what she was doing, and resisted the urge to pull out the Map and stare at the holographic Pho Altis. That wouldn't accomplish anything and would just make him sad again.

Betsy had finished eating her dinner and was a little way off, playing a game with Bergen and giggling freely, obviously not thinking of the mountains at all. She was tossing Jules's fedora through the air trying to get it to land on top of Bergen, who was standing about fifteen feet away from her with his arms pinned to his sides like a post. Already Betsy had been trying for ten minutes and had yet to find the mark, although she had come close several times.

Jules shook his head. "Ring toss with a troll and an old hat," he snorted, shaking his head. "Now I've seen everything."

Bergen didn't seem to mind. "Better than tryin' to throw *me* into the hat," he said with a shrug. He carried the hat back to Betsy, and then scampered back to his position, waiting for her next attempt.

Betsy took aim and let the hat fly. The fedora soared through the air, and this time landed directly on top of Bergen, completely engulfing him. "I did it!" Betsy cried with glee. "Jules, were you watching?"

"I saw. I bet you can't do it again."

"We'll see about that." Betsy skipped over and plucked the hat off of Bergen, but the troll was too quick for her. He reached up and grabbed hold of the rim and pulled, and soon the two of them were embroiled in a tug-of-war, with Jules's poor hat getting the worst of it. Bergen and Betsy laughed as they tugged against each other. Time seemed to stop. Eventually Bergen's small fingers slipped and Betsy flew back, landing on her backside and breaking into a fit of hysterics. At that same moment, something fluttered out of the hat and fell to the ground.

"What's that?" asked Jules, just relieved that his beloved fedora hadn't ripped in half.

"It's a piece of paper," Betsy said. She reached down, picked it up, and unfolded it. "It must've been inside the hat."

"I put it there to make it fit better," Jules remembered. "It slips behind that little flap that goes around the inside of the rim. Can you fold it up and put it back?"

"There's something written on it," Betsy said, frowning.

"What? Let me see."

Jules came over and took the page from Betsy. Sure enough, there was some writing on it in a rough cursive script. Why hadn't he noticed that earlier? He vaguely recalled how dark it was in the Klepner house when he had folded those loose sheets into strips and stuffed them inside the hat so it would stay above his ears. Now curious, he reached inside the hat and removed the other papers from behind the flap. These, too, had writing on them.

Bergen was sitting on the ground, watching them with disinterest.

"What do they say?" Betsy asked.

"You better read them," Jules said, handing her all the pages. "I'm not a very good reader. You're probably better at it than I am."

"But you're older than I am," Betsy protested, pushing them back.

"Yes, but I have dyslexia. Do you know what that means?"

"No."

"It means I have trouble reading words the right way. I mix up the letters and put them in the wrong order. So, for example, your name is Betsy, spelled B-E-T-S-Y. If I saw that written on a page, I might read it as 'Tesby' or 'Steyb' or even 'Etsby.'"

Betsy giggled. "Etsby. That's funny."

"No, it's not. I can't help it."

"I'm sorry I laughed." Then, after a pause, Betsy asked, "Does it hurt?"

"That's a silly question. Why would it hurt? I'm not sick or anything. I just can't read well."

"I meant when other kids make fun of you."

"Oh." Jules sat back down on the grass. "Sometimes, I guess. I'm mostly used to it now, but sometimes it still stings a little bit. They think I'm stupid because of the way I read, but I'm not stupid at all. I'm as smart as they are; I'm just a little different, that's all. My dad used to say I have some quirks. I really miss him, my dad. Do you have any quirks?"

"I don't like the sound of people eating lettuce. It makes me shiver. Does that count?"

"Yeah, I guess so." He paused. "I'm getting better at it," Jules continued after a moment. "Reading, I mean. But I still have trouble with handwriting like this."

He held out the papers once more, and this time Betsy took them. She smoothed them out and put them in a pile. As the sun began to set and streaks of red and yellow formed across the sky, she began to read silently to herself.

"Well?" he said after a minute of quiet, getting impatient. "What is it?"

Betsy frowned, collecting her thoughts. "I'm not sure. I think these are a couple of pages from someone's diary."

"Really?"

"Yes. Let me try to put them in order." She rifled through the pages and reorganized them, then wordlessly skimmed through them once more. Finally, she said, "It doesn't make any sense. It talks about places and things I've never heard of and sounds as if someone made it up."

"Does it say who wrote it?"

"No. But it mentions someone named Mortimer."

Jules felt the blood drain from his face. "Mortimer? Are you sure? That was my Dad's name."

"Here, I'll read you the first part. Maybe you'll understand it better than I do."

March 18

Mortimer came to see me today. He hasn't changed a bit. I never expected to see him again after what happened between us. He had a sharp look in his eyes. He told me Thisted visited him last night and told him there was some trouble in the Forest that he needed to make right. I told him that Thisted was a lying scoundrel who couldn't be trusted. He didn't care. 'Klep,' he said, 'I need your help. I can't do this alone.' He asked me to put our differences aside and go on this one last adventure together. It's been almost ten years since we've been in that World, and now that I have my own family I can't run off whenever the mood comes over me. He just doesn't understand responsibility, never did, or at least not in the same way most people do. But even after all this time, I'm unable to say no to his face. I told him I'd think about it.

Jules's hands began to tremble as the words sank in. This was about his father . . . and what, exactly, did it mean? Who could have written this? *Klep* . . . Could that have been Mr. Klepner? Could they have been more than just acquaintances and casual neighbors, but old friends who shared a secret past? He was suddenly aware of how little he truly knew about his father, that he must've had a whole different life before Jules was born. He intuitively knew this was something important, tried to focus. "Don't stop, Betsy," he whispered urgently. "Read more. Please."

"Okay." She wet her lips and continued:

March 21

I haven't seen Mortimer this happy in years. He's nearly all packed, and it looks like he's ready to fight an army with or without my help. He even found that ugly fedora he always liked to wear so much. I think there's more to what Thisted told him, but he refuses to give me any details. Same old Mortimer. I wish he had never looked at that damned Map in the first place. I told him I'd go with him one more time, but this was it.

"There's more," Betsy said. "But it's confusing. It goes on about castles and knights and things like that. What do you think it means?"

"That's okay," Jules said. "I've heard enough." It all made sense now. He advanced on Bergen, who was still sitting in the grass near the spring. "My *father* was the last person who looked at the Map before me? So he's the one who died and caused your world to fall apart? Thisted should have told me," he continued, his voice rising. "You should have told me."

Bergen shrugged. "It was before my time. What difference does it make who it was, anyway?"

"It makes all the difference in the world!" His voice dripped with anger, betrayal. Disappointment, too. "I have a right to know about my father. Some friend you are! If you don't know why this is important to me, then I guess you don't know anything about me at all. And to think I trusted you. Don't you think that's something I should have known?"

Bergen shrugged again, but didn't say anything.

"So I guess my father was the guy who defeated Count Barchmod and rescued the Copper Princess all those years ago? That's probably where they were headed when that Mr. Klepner wrote that diary."

Bergen nodded.

"And don't you think that maybe the count kidnapped my mom as a way to get revenge?"

Bergen looked at Jules blankly. "That's irrelevant now. What difference does it make?"

"Irrelevant? What difference? I thought you were my friend, Bergen. A friend would've told me something like that."

"I'm sorry, boy. I didn't mean—"

"If I had known about this earlier, maybe I could have kept her safe. After we first met, you should've told me she was in danger. That we were *all* in danger. That would have been the right thing to do. The sort of thing that friends do for each other. The count has probably been watching my family for years, looking for a chance to get even. Spying on us."

"I said I'm sorry. Thisted said—"

"I don't care what that nasty mountain troll said. You could have told me anyway. I thought you were my friend." He nearly spit out the last word. "I think I want to be alone now. Just go away, would you?"

"But—"

"Just go. Get out of here."

Bergen got up and scuffled off across the clearing and into the forest. Betsy shifted her gaze between the two of them until the troll vanished from view. Then she stamped her foot in frustration.

"I think you're being unfair, Jules," she said, crossing her arms across her chest. "Bergen's your best friend and has been helping you this whole time, and I don't know what it will take for you to realize it. If you're going to act like this, I—I don't want to be with you, either." She snorted, flicked her head, then turned and walked in the direction Bergen had just gone. "Wait up," she called. "I'm coming with you."

"Good riddance," Jules mumbled. "Did you hear me?" he screamed. "I said good riddance." Then he curled up on his jacket and fell into a dreamless sleep.

CHAPTER 11

Tunnels and Caves

Jules woke the next morning as the sun's rays came over the mountains. He sat up and looked around. He was alone. Instantly the details of the previous night's argument flooded back. The anger, the yelling. The accusations. He realized he was stupid to say the things he did. "It's because I'm not used to having friends," he said aloud. But his regret didn't change the basic fact that Betsy and Bergen hadn't returned after he'd driven them away.

How far could they have gone in the dark? They were probably asleep in the woods not far away. He cupped his hands around his mouth and called out. "Bergen? Betsy? *Burrrrr*-gen?"

No answer. "Well, I guess I better go find them," he said with a sigh. "After all, it's my fault they're gone."

He walked through the woods in the general direction Bergen and Betsy had disappeared, pausing every now and then to give a quick shout. About a quarter mile away the forest ended at the edge of a sandy plain that gradually sloped upward until reaching the base of the neighboring foothills. He shouted again, and once more there was no reply.

He continued forward, marveling at the sight of this odd landscape, wondering what to do next. Where could they have gotten to? *Think, Jules, think,* he admonished himself. He struck the side of his head with his palm in an attempt to rattle his brain into action. This only made him dizzy, and he sat down in the soft dirt. A small cloud of dust spread around his ankles. Absentmindedly, he picked up a handful of dirt and released it, watching the wind carry it away.

The dirt—of course! He glanced around. Behind him, leading along the ridge, was the familiar tread of his own footprints. He saw some bird prints, and some strange hoofmarks, but nothing that resembled Bergen's large, flat feet or Betsy's shoes. So they hadn't come this way.

I must have taken a wrong turn, or perhaps didn't turn when I should have. Jules backtracked until he located the point where his tracks diverged from a half-dozen other sets of prints, including some clearly left by a woodland troll with big feet. He turned in this new direction, which led toward a narrow pass between two nearby hills. Now sure he was on the right path, he started to run. "I'm coming, I'm coming," he called out. "Wait for—"

He stopped suddenly. He had reached the edge of a deep hole in the earth and had almost fallen in. He hadn't seen it until it was nearly too late.

Sure enough, the footsteps led directly into the hole. *It must be an underground cave,* Jules thought. *The roof probably caved in, and Bergen and Betsy must've fallen through.* Now that the mystery behind his friends' disappearance was solved, Jules felt relief wash over him. It was just a matter of retrieving them.

He craned his neck just enough so his head was over the hole and looked down into the darkness. "Hello!" he cried out, more confident this time. "Taken a spill, did you? Well, no fear, I'll get you out, we'll be back on the road in no time."

There was still no response.

"Bergen?" he called down. "Betsy? Hello?"

They must not be able to hear me, Jules thought. *I wonder how far it is to the bottom.* He leaned over the hole as far as he could and peered down, but his gaze was unable to pierce the gloom. Without thinking, he picked up a palm-sized stone and dropped it into the pit. Then he realized what he had done and held his breath, hoping he didn't accidentally pelt his friends in the head. A few seconds later, though, he heard a dim thud as the rock hit ground, and he exhaled a sigh of relief.

He tried to estimate the distance from the time it had taken for the sound to reach him, and wished he had thought clearly enough to count the seconds. Was it twenty feet? Thirty?

How long does it take for a rock to fall that far, anyway? Regardless, it was definitely too far to jump without risking turning an ankle or worse. Hopefully Betsy's fall didn't end that way.

"Of course! The rope!" he said. "I've carried it all this way, and I've completely forgotten about it. Jules, you really are a fool."

He opened his pack and grabbed the rope that had been packed there by Algard and Alesund. After tying one end to an old tree stump a few yards away, he tossed the other end down the hole.

"Here, now," Jules cried into the chasm. "Climb out, that's right. One, two, one, two. It's old Jules to the rescue, once again!" He paused. "Quickly now, or there won't be any dinner tonight." Again there was no answer.

"Perhaps they're injured," he said. "Or can't hear me. I guess I'll have to go down there after all." Taking a deep breath, Jules grabbed the rope with both hands and slowly lowered himself into the hole. He used the hand-under-hand method, letting his legs hang below him, and this went just fine until he reached the end of the rope. There he hung, feet dangling in midair without the strength to pull himself back up, when he suddenly lost his grip and fell into the darkness.

Squealing, Jules landed on the ground with a hard thump. He had fallen just a short distance. Looking up, he saw the end of the rope swaying back and forth about eight feet off the ground, well out of reach. No matter. Working together, the three of them could figure out a way to climb out. He was sure of it. But before that happened, he'd have to find Betsy and Bergen first, wherever they might be.

The light was faint down in the hole, and it took a few moments for Jules's eyes to adjust to the dark. He discovered that he was all alone in a large domed cavern shaped vaguely like the inside of an upside down bowl. The floor was littered with loose debris, small rocks mostly, that had quite clearly fallen when Betsy and Bergen broke through the roof far above. Yet there were no signs of his missing friends. Where could they have gone? Had they been struck by some of the falling boulders and were now lying in one of the gloomy corners of this cavern, hurt and unconscious? Or was it possible he had made a terrible mistake, and they hadn't even fallen down here at all? He scrambled around looking for clues, soon discovering a series of scuff marks in the dirt.

"Look at this!" he said aloud. "That's Bergen's footprint, I'd recognize it anywhere." And that one over there looked like it could be Betsy's. But what were those other ones? He tried to make sense of them, but they were unlike any he'd ever seen. They were round, like those of a large animal, but instead of a hoof they had toes—six on each foot, in fact. Regardless of what made the footprints, one thing was clear: Betsy and Bergen weren't alone down here in the dark, and they could very well be in trouble.

"It looks like they all walked off in that direction," Jules began to say before catching himself mid-sentence. Someone— or something—might discover him if he continued to talk aloud, and he better be careful. He was all alone now; he'd have to do a better job watching out for himself. He peered across the cavern, following the trail of footprints with his eyes. Then in the shadows he noticed an ominous dark spot he hadn't seen before. It was the entrance to a narrow passageway. Twisting his head around, he discovered another similar passage leading in the opposite direction. He had been wrong; this wasn't an isolated hole in the ground that his friends had accidentally stumbled upon, but possibly a part of an entire network of tunnels and caves that might lead for miles under the earth.

So there it was. Bergen and Betsy were lost underground, possibly even captured and led away by some mysterious subterranean terror that most likely breathed fire and ate boys for breakfast. Jules stood up straight and took a deep breath. This was no time to feel sorry for himself; his imagination would have to wait for another time. He looked up again at the swinging piece of rope. There was only one course. He would have to try to rescue his friends or be captured himself. "Well, then, onwards!" he said, and did as he was told.

Jules entered the passage and was immediately enveloped by a darkness so deep he could not even see his fingers pinch his own nose, although he was still able to feel it. He resisted the temptation to use one of his few remaining matches; he didn't have a candle or torch, and it would just burn out after a few seconds. It would be better to hold onto his remaining stock until they were most needed. He extended his arm and took a few lateral steps until he touched the wall. It was cold, smooth.

With his fingers still grazing the wall, he inched forward, hoping not to bump into anything. Gradually he felt his other senses sharpen. He smelled the putrid scent of stagnant water; he heard some small animal pawing the dirt a few yards ahead, probably a rat or mouse like the one that had tormented him for months in the family store. Something brushed his face and he heard wings beating. Jules jumped in fright, but whatever it was flew off and never returned.

He continued forward in the dark. After some time, though, he thought he could begin to make out the contours of the walls. *Just imagining things*, he thought, but then as he advanced further and curved around a bend, he noticed a dim light ahead, from a junction with another passage. He jumped back into the darkness, afraid he'd stumbled upon some underground city of the six-toed creatures and would be discovered.

He waited in silence for a few minutes, but heard nothing other than his pounding heartbeat and another rodent pawing the dirt. Finally satisfied that he was alone, he sneaked forward as quietly as he could. He reached the junction and poked his head around the edge of the corridor, tentatively, just in case something—or someone—was there.

It was empty, but Jules now saw the source of the dim light that illuminated the tunnel. A thick vein of fluorescent mineral was embedded in the rock of the tunnel walls and glowed with a soft blue-green tint. He couldn't tell if the glowing rock was a natural phenomenon or had been applied like a coat of paint.

Regardless, this was obviously a main passage, for it was wider than the tunnel he'd just come through and contained many more of the animal-like footprints going in both directions. After studying the ground for a short time, Jules discovered Bergen's distinctive prints. They went off to the left. There was no indication of Betsy.

Now would start the hard part of this rescue attempt. Once he started off down this new, wider tunnel, he'd be exposed in the light, and he'd be unable to hide in a niche or corner if one of the six-toed creatures came by. Jules paused and listened; there were no voices or footsteps. The creatures that had dragged Bergen and Betsy off—if that was what had happened—must be far ahead by now. He berated himself for yelling at Bergen and chasing him away from the camp. But Bergen could take care of himself; he was tiny and could sneak away safely when no one was watching. No, Jules was more concerned about Betsy. Betsy was just a girl, and shouldn't even have been here in the first place. He should've taken her back to the tunnel to the Klepner house when he had a chance. Now she was his responsibility, and he had lost her. He had better find her, and fast. Jules gulped hard and started off.

The tunnel seemed to have no end. It stayed more or less on a straight course, descending deeper into the ground, until leveling off a half mile or so later. The fluorescent walls led him onward. Every now and then he passed smaller passages that branched off to one side or the other. Few of these tunnels contained the fluorescent rock, and thus most led into darkness.

He ignored these spurs and remained along the main passageway, following the trail of footprints. On and on he went. Periodically he stepped in a cold stream or puddle, which startled him, but they were only a few inches deep and did nothing but get his sneakers wet. He marched on in silence, hearing no sound except for his own breathing. He didn't know how long he continued like this. It could have been an hour; it could have been all night.

Soon the passage began to rise, and Jules continued forward as best he could. But at last the slope flattened, the corridor turned a corner, and he came to a large wooden door, blocking the way. Slowly Jules crept up to the door and grasped the handle. It didn't turn; the door was locked.

Just then he heard voices. Someone—or something—was walking down the tunnel toward him! Without time to think, he ducked into the nearest side passage, which was pitch-black and smelled funny. He pressed himself against the wall and tried not to move.

"…completely caved in," said a deep voice. "Broke a hole in the roof, and jumped right through."

"Could've been an accident," a second voice said. "Wouldn't be the first time. Just last month I heard there'd been a rockslide in A-17. It was blocked for a week before they could get it cleared. The tunnels are falling apart right and left."

"Not this time. I *saw*."

"What?"

"A rope."

"Really!"

"Yup. Nasty buggers left it hanging down through the hole in the roof. Didn't even bother to stow it away. Like they didn't care if we saw it."

A pause. "You serious?"

"Yeah. But we cut it down and took it back with us. Now they're trapped down here with us, the lot of them."

"What do you think they are?"

"They're Above-Grounders, of course—definitely Above-Grounders. Probably got tiny beady eyes from staring at the miserable yellow thing all day. Bet they stand straight up, too, not used to tunnels at all."

The two creatures passed the dark corridor where Jules was hiding and he heard them stop in front of the wooden door, their breathing loud and raspy.

"I say we catch the buggers and eat 'em, that's what I'd do. Wonder what they taste like."

There was a laugh, cold and heartless. "Tired of eating rat, Noldar? You'd eat anything, wouldn't you! You don't even know what they're made of. They could give you a stomachache, or worse. Remember you tried to eat that stinky black-and-white striped furry thing you found scurrying along the tunnels last year? Your face swelled up like a balloon."

"Allergic reaction. Could've happened to anyone."

"And the time that—"

"Okay, I get your point."

"I'll stick to juicy rat, when I can get it. Now where is that key?" There was a jingling sound.

"Why are the doors locked, anyway?" Noldar asked. "Never seen so much security."

"Idiot!" There was a faint slap, followed by an 'ow!' "Do you think they came down here by chance? They're spies, I warrant. Spies or thieves, perhaps. There's bound to be more coming, too. Maybe even a full-fledged invasion. That's orders from the top, lock all the doors until this mess is over. Now where did I put that key?"

Jules worked up his courage and peeked around the edge of the junction. He saw two stocky creatures, both covered with coarse black hair and wearing official-looking uniforms. They had long arms, thick as tree trunks, which hung down past their knees.

"Are all the doors to be locked?" Noldar asked. "Even *hers?*" He nodded in the direction of the passage where Jules was hiding. Jules felt the blood drain from his face and quickly jumped back before he was seen.

The first creature laughed, a hideous sound that made Jules shudder. "Would you go lock it? Not me, I wouldn't! That way is safe, door or no door. *She'll* get them if they go down that way. Ah, here it is!" The lock clicked and the door squeaked open.

"How many do you think there were again?" Noldar asked in his distinctive scratchy voice. Then the door slammed shut, cutting off the rest of the conversation.

Jules exhaled hard, his heart beating. After a few minutes, once he thought it was safe, he left the side passage and approached the wooden door. He grasped the handle and pulled. No luck. It was again locked.

What a mess! He, Jules, trapped underground all alone, and thought to be a spy, quite likely part of the first wave of an invasion. What was he to do? He couldn't go forward, and he couldn't go back, not with the rope cut down and with these gorilla-like subterranean creatures probably swarming through the tunnels searching for him. He was also exhausted. Time had seemed to stand still since he descended into the earth, and he had no idea how long he'd been walking through this underground maze. Trying to ignore the harsh stench, he moved a few yards deeper into the darkened side passage and sank down on the ground to figure out what to do next.

Not too long later he felt something tugging on his pants-leg.

Jules opened his eyes with alarm. "Bergen?" he said, unable to see anything in the shadows.

For once Jules was right about something, for in front of him stood not just Bergen, but Betsy as well. "Wake up, if yer not dead or bewitched," the troll said.

"Bergen!" he cried. "Betsy! Thank goodness I've found you!"

"Hi, Jules," said Betsy.

"Thought you'd never git up," Bergen said. "You sleep like a cave troll."

"I wasn't sleeping. I was . . . thinking."

"Is that what they call it these days?"

"Oh, forget about that," Jules said. "I'm so glad to see you both. I'm really sorry, Bergen. I shouldn't have said the things I did back in the forest. It's just that I miss my father so much. He wasn't afraid of anything. He'd go rescue my mom straight off and nothing would be able to stop him. He wouldn't have been afraid of Alexis, and he certainly wouldn't be hiding scared in an underground tunnel like I am. Will you forgive me?"

"It's okay, boy. I know you didn't mean none of it."

"Now that we've found each other, can we get out of here and back into the fresh air?" asked Betsy. "I don't like these tunnels one bit. They give me the creeps, and some of them smell really bad."

"I wish we could," Jules said. "But I think that's going to be a problem."

"Why? What's wrong?"

"Well, for one thing, we're not alone down here. The tunnels are swarming with these creatures that look a bit like gorillas, and they don't sound very friendly."

"We know," Bergen said. "We've seen 'em. They're called the Marochi. A pack of 'em came to investigate after we broke through the cavern roof. We just managed to sneak away without bein' seen. Been busy tryin' to avoid 'em since."

"It's even worse than you think," Jules said. "I heard one of them say they cut down the rope I used to follow you down here."

Bergen groaned. "Looks like we're stuck."

"I don't want to spend the rest of my life down here," Betsy whined.

"Don't cry, Betsy," Jules soothed. "I think they go to the surface at night to hunt for food, so there has to be another way out of here. I think it's through that door, but it's locked and we don't have a key."

"What do you think we should do?" Bergen asked.

"Well . . . I'm not sure, but there might be another possibility. I heard two ape-men say something about a door at the end of this passage that hasn't been locked yet. Maybe it goes to the same place. What do you think? Do you want to try?"

"I just want to get out of here," Betsy wailed.

"We could get lost," Jules pointed out. "And it could be— dangerous."

"I don't care," Betsy said.

"What do you think your father would do?" Bergen asked.

Jules didn't pause before answering. "He'd go down the tunnel without thinking twice about it. He always said it's always better to take matters into your own hands than wait around for something to happen."

"Then that's what we should do," Bergen said. "Lead on!"

So Jules started down the side passage, with Betsy alongside and Bergen scurrying at their feet. They stumbled ahead in the dark, feeling their way with their hands. The stench became more pronounced, hinting at terrible foul things, but just when he thought he couldn't go any further without retching, the narrow tunnel opened up into a wide cavern, the walls once again glowed blue-green, and the offensive smell cleared. He took half a dozen deep breaths and felt better almost at once.

"I don't know what made that stink in the passage," Bergen said, "but I'll bet anything it lives here, and I wouldn't be surprised if it was watchin' us now. Anything that smells that bad can't be good."

"I think you're right." Jules glanced around. A stagnant pool of ooze filled the center of the cavern. As he watched, a few large bubbles emerged and popped, spewing green slime. Around the edges of the cavern, six different passages led off into the darkness, not counting the one they'd just come through.

Which direction to take now, he wondered. He realized that the others were depending on him, and the pressures of leadership weighed heavily. He picked up a stone and threw it into the pool. It made a hollow *plop*, which echoed ominously through the chamber.

"I think there's a faint light coming from one of the tunnels," Bergen said. "It's the second one from the left."

"I think I can see it, too," Betsy said. "It must be the way out. Let's go."

"Careful," said Jules, grabbing her elbow. "I don't like this place. And if Bergen is right about something being in here with us, I don't want to be taken by surprise. Let's do this slowly."

Betsy nodded and held out her hand, which Jules took in his own. They proceeded forward, stepping lightly, trying to make as little noise as possible.

The cavern was lit dimly with the center in shadow, where the light from the glowing walls could not reach. To Jules it was as if he was walking through the streets at midnight, which he had done once when he couldn't sleep, went outside, and became temporarily lost. It reminded him of his adventure at the Klepner House, particularly his descent down the stairs to the basement in the dark, holding his breath with each squeak of the steps. His senses were heightened; each drip of water and scratch of the rock echoed in his mind, causing him to jump at the imagined danger.

He squeezed Betsy's hand as they matched footsteps. They continued on, into the darkness. Now the black pool was before them. The air smelled stale here, like raw cabbage that had been left out in the sun too long. Avoiding the water, they crossed over a stretch of bare rock, stepping past great crystalline stalagmites that rose from the ground like a forest of branchless trees. A sappy coat of slime dripped slowly along the walls. Yellow bones were scattered across the ground, some with deep notches carved into them. Betsy stepped on one, breaking the quiet with a hard snapping sound that set Jules's heart pounding.

Now they were past the pool, out of the shadows. Up ahead, the lit tunnel beckoned. They were home free. Jules released Betsy's hand, hitched the backpack higher on his back. "Come on," he said confidently, his voice echoing through the chamber.

Bergen first heard the hiss from behind. He turned with a frightened squeal.

"It's just a scorpion," Jules said, looking down at a small shadow near his feet. He stomped, hard, making a sickly crunching sound. "I guess everything is a little scary when you're less than a foot tall."

But Bergen was looking in a different direction altogether. "No—what's *that?*" he said, pointing back toward the pool. Jules turned, and felt a rush of panic rise inside of him.

For emerging out of the water was an ancient terror, a scorpion the size of an ox. As it moved slowly toward them, its huge jewel-encrusted claws clicked open and shut in the rhythm of a Brazilian samba.

Jules heard Betsy scream. He tried to run, but whether due to fear or the mesmerizing Latin beat, his legs were frozen.

The giant scorpion hissed like a snake, scissoring her claws open and shut, and studied Jules with an unwavering eye. Jules trembled, still unable to move, and the scorpion queen hissed again and halted just a few feet before him. "I am the fear that keeps you awake at night," the scorpion queen whispered. "I am the end of the road. I am Mesetat the Seizer, Mesetat the Stinger." She inched closer. "You are not Marochi. What are you?"

"I—I am just a boy."

"A boy?" Mesetat repeated. Then something awoke in her long memory, and she smiled, at least as much as a scorpion can smile. The effect made Jules shiver. "Human, yessss, a human boy," she hissed. "It has been so long, so very long. But Mesetat remembers, yessss, she does, she remembers. More than anything, she remembers the *smell*. Nothing smells as bad as a human boy."

"She isn't one to talk," Bergen muttered, waving his hand in front of his nose.

The monster hissed and began to inch slowly forward. Jules was too focused on the spellbinding beat of the snapping claws to notice her movement. "But I'm glad you are here, because I have a debt to repay to you, human boy."

"Wh—what do you mean?" asked Jules, who didn't quite like the sound of that at all.

"I was banished here because of a human boy," she replied, inching closer. "But that was a long time ago, a very long time ago. Ancient history. I don't expect that you are interested in that at all. Tell me what you have come for; perhaps I can help you. Fame? Fortune? Knowledge? Why have you come to Mesetat?"

"Please, it was an accident. We just want to find a way out."

"A way out! There *is* no way out except past Mesetat."

Throughout this exchange, the giant scorpion had continued to creep closer and closer to Jules, until she stood just inches away from the hypnotized boy. "And now, I am getting tired of this dull conversation and of you too, child. You are not very interesting at all, and I have much more important things to do. I am afraid that your time is *up*." Mesetat opened one of her claws and slowly brought it toward Jules's head. Light glittered and reflected off the jewels embedded in her claw, momentarily blinding him.

"That's not good," Bergen said. "Come on, boy, snap out of it!"

At that moment Jules felt a sudden sharp pain on his arm, breaking him from the trance.

"Ow!" he cried. He looked over at Betsy, whose thumb and forefinger were clenched firmly around his forearm. "Will you *please* stop pinching me?"

"Just run!" Betsy cried, letting go. Whether it was the blinding flash of light or Betsy's sharp pinch, or perhaps some rediscovered inner strength, Jules had regained the use of his legs. He turned and ran like he had never run before.

There was a soft hissing sound from behind. Mesetat lunged after them, her jewel-encrusted claws clicking like a typewriter as she scuttled along the black rock.

Jules ran, leading Betsy and Bergen toward the lit passage. Past rock, through burning streams. He glanced behind. The scorpion scurried forward, gaining ground. He gasped and was nearly overcome by the putrid smell of rotting flesh. He had run through the cavern and had entered the tunnel at the far end.

Then he tripped over a small rock in the middle of the tunnel and fell on his face. He heard his pants tear at the knee, and he felt a sharp pain in his leg. "Go, go!" he yelled to Betsy as she ran past him. "Don't stop!"

She stopped anyway. "Come on, come on," she begged, tugging anxiously on his shirt. "Jules, you have to get up!"

"I can't," Jules started to say, but then looked up and saw a wooden frame edging the tunnel walls ahead. The inner door, and it was wide open! He scrambled to his feet. "Quick!" he called to Betsy. "We're almost there!" He sprinted ahead until he had passed the threshold. Betsy followed immediately afterward and continued running down the corridor. Jules turned and started to push the door closed, even as he saw Bergen running through the tunnel toward him. The door was stuck! No, it was just a stone jamming it open. Jules kicked the rock away. The door swung easily now. "Hurry!" he shouted. "I'm shutting it!"

"Wait for me!" Bergen cried, and then he was through.

Jules swung the door closed, but he was just a little too late. The scorpion had caught them; Mesetat's claw had slipped between the door and the frame before he was able to completely shut it and was slowly ratcheting the door open.

Jules strained, pushing with his shoulder, trying to dislodge the claw. He felt his muscles weaken. Surely his strength would run out before Mesetat would tire; it was just a matter of—

"Over there!" Betsy shouted.

He turned. There in the corner leaned an old broom. He had a sudden flashback: a broom could be a weapon in a pinch. "Get it, get it!" he screamed.

Betsy rushed over and took the broom in her hands. She reached out with it. Still pressing against the door with his hip, Jules grabbed the end of the wooden handle, pulling it away from her. He jabbed the pole through the open crack of the door, poking the scorpion queen in the eyes, again and again. She hissed and hissed, but didn't retreat. Jules felt the pressure on the door increase.

Then: "Betsy! The matches! They're in my backpack. Quick!"

Jules slid his arms out of the straps and let it fall to the floor. He heard Betsy rummaging around behind him and then felt a small box press against his palm.

"Here it is," she said.

"Light one, light one!" Jules cried out. "Hurry."

"I don't know how. My parents—"

"Just do it!"

Betsy pulled the matchbox out of his hand and fumbled to push it open. After what seemed like ages, Jules heard a scrape and smelled the sharp aroma of sulfur burning.

"I did it," Betsy said. "But I just don't see what good—"

Still poking the broom handle through the crack, Jules angled the sweeping end toward the thin flame and lit a few straw whiskers on fire. Soon the entire bottom part of the broom was engulfed in flames. The orange blaze licked Jules's fingers, and momentarily blinded him after spending so long in the dark of the tunnels.

Flipping the broom like a baton, Jules shoved the torch end through the narrow gap between the door and the frame, smacking Mesetat in the face. He felt her withdraw in surprise. He pushed the handle through a second time, and now there was a high-pitched wail. Instinctively the scorpion queen drew back; Jules tossed the broom through the door and slammed the door shut. The latch locked with a loud click. Mesetat threw herself at the door with all her weight, and screeched with anger. But the door held. They were safe.

Jules fell on the ground, trembling. "We made it," he gasped, then glanced at his partners, who were engulfed in a cloud of dark smoke. "Bergen! Your hair! It's on fire!" Quickly Jules tore off his jacket and threw it on top of the little troll, patting at the flames until they were extinguished.

Jules lifted off the jacket. "Bergen? Are you all right?" There stood the troll, his forehead and scalp blackened by the flames, looking bewildered and a little shocked, but otherwise unhurt.

"That's the last time you chance leavin' me behind," the troll scolded. "I could've gotten eaten by that thing! Next time we face a giant scorpion, I'm ridin' on yer shoulder. Or, better yet, inside yer backback, where it's safe." He glared at his two friends. "What is it? Why are you lookin' at me like that?"

"Oh, dear," Betsy said. "It's all gone."

"What?"

"Your hair's burned off." Betsy giggled, unable to help herself. "Your head looks like a fried goose egg."

Bergen patted the top of his head and winced when he touched his bare scalp, which was lightly charred. "It's not funny," he said with a grimace. "I can't go through life like this."

"Oh, it'll grow back," Jules said. "The important thing is that you're okay. I'll make you a hat or something." He reached down and lifted up his friend, placing him on his shoulder.

"Later. Now we have but one choice—to go forward! I certainly hope we chose the right tunnel."

CHAPTER 12

The Underground City

They continued through the musty passage. The light grew brighter as they walked, reflecting off the thick sap that dripped down the rock walls like maple syrup. They slowed their pace, careful not to make any unnecessary sounds, not knowing what dangers might lie ahead. In this way they sneaked along the final stretch of the tunnel, until it unexpectedly flared wide and ended at a T-intersection with another corridor. Jules jumped back several yards, pulling Betsy with him.

"Stay here," he warned her.

"Why?" she bristled.

Jules sighed. Even after their long journey together, he felt obliged to protect her, to keep her from harm to the best of his ability. She was, after all, younger by several years and he was responsible for her safety. "Because I said so." He realized that made him sound overbearing, like adults who only want quiet from children who just want noise, and sighed again. He placed his hand on her shoulder. "I'm not going ahead without you, promise. I'll take a look first and make sure it's clear."

She nodded, her eyes wide. "Be careful."

"Bergen," he said. A statement, not a question.

Bergen hopped off Jules's shoulder, landing in the crook of Betsy's elbow, where he sat with his feet dangling. She scratched behind the troll's mammoth ears, which made him coo softly.

"He'll stay with you. But I'll just be a moment, promise."

He stepped forward until he reached the edge of the junction, then stopped. Twisting his head, Jules could see Betsy standing near the tunnel wall, waiting. He waved and flashed her the thumbs-up signal before turning away and leaning forward to listen. The persistent low-pitched hum of machinery knifed through the air. He took another few steps and peeked around the corner.

At first, Jules had to remind himself that he was still underground. He stood on the edge of an immense cavern, the walls of which extended far upward to form a high-topped dome. The roof was far above—so far, in fact, that it was nearly out of sight. Ahead of him stretched a great underground city, with square clay buildings separated by walking paths or streets.

He had come out on what was evidently a ring-road rimming the outer wall of the cavern, encircling the city like a belt. Glass lanterns were suspended over the ground on long curved poles, glowing with pale blue light. From his position, it was as if he was loitering on the deserted corner of a wide avenue on the edge of town, waiting for the bus.

In the distance, near a cluster of buildings, companies of ape-soldiers trotted in formation, wearing matching uniforms and carrying shields and long spears. No doubt these troops were patrolling the city to stem the approaching invasion. Jules glanced back at Betsy, silhouetted in the shadows, and shuddered. Only they knew the truth, that there was no invasion, just a lost, frightened boy and girl—and pint-sized troll!—doing their best to get unlost and to the surface where they belonged.

He studied the scene before him. The enormity of their task overwhelmed him. They'd have to navigate through the Marochi city without being detected by the troops, to the other side of the dome, where hopefully there'd be a way out of this underground maze. How was it possible? It might be easier to simply turn around and take their chances with Mesetat a second time and try to locate another way out. No; that way was closed. It would have to be forward. If only his father was here. He'd come up with a plan lickety-split, and still find the time to crack a joke or two to make Jules smile. Jules would have to figure something out on his own; Betsy was depending on him to get them home safely. But what?

Over the continuous rumble of machinery, Jules heard some noise from down the ring-road. He jumped back into the tunnel, unseen. Three or four Marochi drew near. They were slender and about Jules's height, and were laughing and teasing each other as if part of some game. Kids, he realized with a start. Until that moment, he hadn't thought that the Marochi were anything but adult soldiers, but of course there would be children, and old people, too. For a moment he wondered if they had pets, and what sort of animals could live down here, without sunlight in this underground city. Maybe they had six legs, and tails that opened like flowers. In his imagination—

No. He had to focus on the present. He studied the Marochi from the shadows. They wore dark cloaks around their necks that hung to the back of their knees. The youths approached the tunnel tentatively, although they seemed oblivious to Jules's presence just around the corner. He stepped back farther into the shadows and motioned for Betsy and Bergen to be quiet so he could listen to their conversation.

"This is it," one of the young ape-creatures said. "This is the one."

"Okay," said another. "You proved. Can we go now? This tunnel gives me the spooks."

"Not until we walk down it."

Walk down? Jules felt the blood drain from his cheeks. What would he do? He glanced around frantically. There was no place to hide. Once he was detected, Betsy would be found, too. And then what? Would they be tied up, hung upside down from the lampposts to be used as targets in a spear-throwing contest? Handed over to the soldiers to be locked away in a cell somewhere and forgotten? He tried not to think about it, to turn off his imagination. He remained extra still and continued to listen.

"Are you crazy? Let's get out of here."

"Told you, not until we walk it."

"But Mesetat—"

"Forget about that stupid crab."

"Heard she turns Marochi children into zombies."

"Heard she mesmerizes her victims and eats their insides, sucks them out through their stomachs like goo."

"But only if they've been bad."

"Well, it isn't true, no matter what your mama told you," replied the first Marochi, clearly exasperated. "Besides, we're not gonna bother her. We're here for something else. Don't you know what's been going on? I heard some of the elders talking. Some . . . *things* entered the tunnels last night." He barely whispered that last part.

"Some . . . *things?*"

"That's what I heard, yup yup."

"From . . . above?"

"Yup yup, from above. They think it's the start of an invasion. That's why the city's so quiet today. Everyone's out hunting for them."

"So . . . why are we here again?"

"To see them for ourselves, of course! I'm tired of being left behind."

"But why here?"

"Think for a moment—if you wanted to infiltrate the city, how would you do it? Not by the main tunnels! Nope!"

"You'd use a tunnel no one uses," said one of the others.

"Exactly! This is the only unguarded entrance. The elders ignore it. They think Mesetat will catch anything that enters her lair. But if they get by her . . . we'll be here waiting for them!"

Jules poked his head out of the mouth of the tunnel, until he had a clear view of the Marochi children. He saw them nod their heads in agreement with that last statement, all except one, the smallest (and presumably the youngest) of the group.

"Um," the young Marochi said in a squeaky voice, "if those above-landers can get past Mesetat, they'd probably have special powers or be great warriors, yes?"

"I guess."

"So wouldn't they be dangerous? All we have are unsharpened spear-sticks."

There was a pause. "Hadn't thought of that. I don't know."

"Shouldn't we—Aaaargh!!"

The young Marochi yelled, for at that moment he caught a glimpse of Jules huddled in the darkness. He had been too careless, and now he had been discovered. Not knowing what to do, he jumped out of the shadows, arms extended, hoping to scare the Marochi in their moment of self-doubt.

It worked. He saw the ape-creatures nearly jump out of their skins, heard them gasp in horror. As they turned to run, Jules darted forward and managed to grab hold of two of their cloaks. He heard the tearing of cloth, the shrieks of surprise, the pounding of feet. Then almost instantly the street was empty and quiet once more, leaving him alone—but not empty-handed, for he had broken the clasps that had held the cloaks in place around their necks.

"This will do quite well," Jules muttered, studying the dark fabric held firmly in each of his hands. A plan had begun to form in his mind. He called softly to Betsy.

"What's that?" she said, motioning to his hands.

"Our way out. Turn around."

He draped one of the capes around her neck, tying the broken clasp together with a bow knot, then stood still while she did the same to him. He breathed, nearly retching from the rancid smell embedded in the cloth. He twisted the cape so it wrapped neatly around his body, obscuring his human form as much as possible, and waited while Betsy did the same.

"An' you thought my old burlap shirt needed replacin'," Bergen noted, shaking his head. "You two look ridiculous. Like a pair of beginner vampires."

"If it helps us escape, I'll wear anything," Betsy replied. She drew the hood over her head. Then, to Jules, she added, "I trust you."

"Come on," he said, pulling on his hood, which flopped over his eyes. "We don't have much time. They may come back."

With their hairless arms and their pale faces disguised, Jules and Betsy set forth along the ring-road. Bergen trotted at their feet, using his superior vision to search for nearby motion that could indicate they'd been detected. At the first intersection, they shifted direction and headed toward the looming city.

They reached the first clay buildings and passed through the narrow streets. Some of the structures were domed, making Jules think of upside down tea cups, with small circular windows cut in them. It was quiet. The young Marochi back at the tunnel had been correct: the settlement appeared empty. Several times they noticed a phalanx of soldiers trotting along a side street, but Jules and Betsy kept their heads down and no attention was paid to them. From time to time they heard bats fluttering overhead. A radio blared jazz from someone's home. A baby cried.

A Marochi woman exited through a door and collided with Jules, dropping a bag of groceries in the street. A circular loaf of bread rolled away like a soccer ball.

"Watch yerselves," she said, glaring.

Jules pulled the cloak tighter around his face. "Yup yup," he shouted, doing his best to lower the pitch of his voice.

As the woman chased down the bread, he grabbed Betsy by the elbow. "Come on," he whispered urgently. He dragged her around the corner, down a smaller street.

"Where's—" he started. He looked behind. Bergen hopped out of the woman's shopping bag, holding a half-chewed piece of fruit.

"Comin', comin'," the troll said, tossing the remains of his snack into the street. "Jus' gettin' my bearings."

That was the closest call. They slipped through the heart of the city, where the buildings were taller and included silver decorative trim, through to the other side, toward the far wall of the cavern. Here the buildings were replaced by large banks of machinery that towered above the ground and growled with a deep hum. So the Marochi were engineers of some sort.

Jules and Betsy navigated through the labyrinth of metal, mesmerized by the flashing lights from all sides. The equipment reminded Jules of old computers, the kind that were said to take up whole rooms by themselves and were fed instructions on punch cards. They continued on, trusting that they were proceeding in the right direction and that it would lead to an exit from this miserable underground world.

Ahead was a sign that read 'AIR CIRCULATION PUMP #6,' whatever that meant. On a nearby metal panel, colored lights blinked and flashed next to a bank of indicator needles. The humming was louder here. Fascinated, Jules paused to try to make sense of the various settings and displays. Then there was a loud thump, and one of the needles started fluctuating wildly.

"That's weird," he said. One of the other needles began inching up. "Hey, Bergen," he started, "did you—"

He glanced around. The little troll was several yards ahead, shoving concrete shards and other debris into a grate a few inches off the ground. Now, dark smoke spilled from the opening, and the machine began to vibrate like a washing machine during the spin cycle.

"What are you doing?" Jules demanded, grabbing the little troll and pulling him away from the grate. "Can't you behave for once?"

Bergen was laughing at his mischief and watched the machine tremble with an open-mouthed grin. "It never hurts to shake things up every now an' then," the troll said, giggling.

"You're unbelievable," Jules said, dropping the troll onto the ground.

Bergen brushed the chalky residue from his shirt. "I'm a troll, a woodland troll at that. And if you don't know what that entails by now, you haven't been payin' close enough attention."

Jules glanced at the nearest control panel. One of the needles had now swung into its red zone. A siren began to sound, a long, deep horn repeating at regular intervals.

"I think you broke it," Betsy said.

"We'd better get out of here. This thing could explode." Jules grabbed Bergen by the nose and jammed him into his jacket pocket. "That'll keep you out of trouble."

"Jules—behind you!" Betsy cried.

Several Marochi guards appeared from the direction of the city. The sounds of more soldiers drawing near echoed against the metal siding all around them. They'd been discovered. Jules grabbed Betsy by the hand, and together they began to run, to run as fast and as hard as they could, in what they hoped was the right direction.

But the maze of equipment went on and on, never ending. They hit a dead end, had to backtrack down a separate corridor. A spear landed near Jules's feet, then another and another. He heard another rumbling sound, more rhythmic than from the machines. Lifting his eyes, he saw a freight train advancing along a set of tracks that cut across their path, blocking the way. They were hemmed in—or were they? Up ahead he spied an open-air car—really, no more than a low platform riding on wheels—and another option occurred to him.

"Betsy!" he yelled. "Follow me!"

Without checking whether she was behind, or even if she had heard his directive, Jules ran forward. He heard the shouts of the Marochi in pursuit. But by now he had nearly reached the train. It whizzed by, seemingly at a hundred miles an hour. He felt the ground vibrating under his feet.

But he didn't hesitate. He continued to run at the train, not stopping, not slowing. Shutting his eyes, he jumped as high and far as he could, hurtling over the edge of the car and onto the platform, onto a hard pile of coal. He had timed his approach perfectly. He barely had a chance to exhale when something hit him in the back, and he sprawled forward.

It was Betsy. She had caught up just in time.

Jules rolled, trying to keep from falling off the other side. The jostling threw Bergen from his pocket. The troll bounced across the coal until he was covered with black dust, but he managed to remain on the platform.

"Betsy, we did it!" Jules cried, sitting up. He pulled off the smelly cloak and helped her do the same. Her dress was torn along the hem, but they were safe, at least for now. He stood and watched as the Marochi troops, still giving chase, disappeared into the distance.

The train left the machinery behind and entered a wide tunnel, eventually slowing until it stopped at an underground station. There was the sound of steam released from the engine.

"I wonder if this is a good place to get off," he said.

"I hear voices," Betsy replied, frowning.

They lay flat against the coal. Jules crawled forward to peek over the edge of the coal bin. A group of Marochi were gathered around the train, unhooking individual cars and sending them down different side tunnels, where they would probably be unloaded. It all seemed routine, until Jules noticed a group of soldiers boarding the train a couple of cars behind them.

"I'll bet they're searching for us," he said. "We better get out of here while we can. Come on, Bergen, we don't have all day."

"I'm comin', I'm comin.'" Bergen, who had been wiping the coal dust from his face with a small handkerchief, hopped into Jules's backpack. Then, as the soldiers were preoccupied with a different rail car, Jules and Betsy slipped off the train and hid in the shadows until they were sure all was clear. They crept toward the station, a rectangular wooden building with a wraparound porch and swinging doors painted red. They hurried to one of the other sides of the building, where they'd be out of sight.

The light was brighter here. Wondering why, Jules looked up and noticed that the roof extended upward several hundred feet, as if the train station was at the bottom of a large grain silo. Rays of sunlight filtered down through what had to be a hole at the top. Maybe this was a way out. He edged to the wall of the tunnel and felt around with his hands. His fingers brushed something hard, cold. A metal rung—the first of many.

An emergency exit, perhaps. He showed Betsy with excitement.

"You'd better go first," he said.

"I don't like ladders," she replied. "They make me afraid."

"Well, you'll have to not be afraid of this one. There's no other way."

She nodded and grasped the first rung, before releasing her hold and giving Jules a quick hug. "Good luck," she said.

He smiled. His arms felt warm from her touch. "I'll see you up top."

Betsy nodded again, and began to climb upward into the silo and toward the light.

He watched her ascend. When she was a few feet above his head, he placed a hand on the lowest rung and started to follow. But they had taken too long; as he took his first steps, he felt a hand grabbing at his shoulder. He screamed and turned. Behind him was a group of soldiers reaching for his arms, his legs—any part of him they could touch. He shook loose and kicked out with his feet. With a sickening crunch, his sneaker connected with the head of the nearest guardsman. For a moment he had space, but then the Marochi pressed ahead once more. The Marochi swiped at him, tugging on his pants, but Jules broke free and climbed quickly.

The Marochi pursued him up into the silo. By the time Jules had climbed thirty or forty feet, the closest guard had pulled to within a handful of rungs. The creature reached up and grabbed onto Jules's backpack and yanked. The tension halted his climb. Releasing the backpack meant losing the Map. He tried to pull loose, but the Marochi's grip was unbreakable. He yelled something indecipherable, trying to work free.

"Jules!" Betsy cried from above. "I'm coming down to help."

"No! Keep climbing. I'll be right behind you."

He glanced up, saw her resume her ascent.

Another tug on his back, hard. Jules felt himself losing his grip on the rung. He wrapped his arms around the metal step, trying to resist the urge to look down.

As the guard strengthened his hold on the backpack, Jules felt the weight and pressure on his back increase further.

"I ... can't ... hold ... on ... much ... longer," he whined, although there was no one to hear him, no one to help him.

Or so Jules thought. For upon hearing his friend's plea, Bergen popped out of the backpack holding the retractable umbrella. He swung it back and forth like a sword, trying to hit the guard, to knock him off. But the umbrella was too big and heavy for a troll of his size, and the guard was easily able to parry his swings and thrusts.

When Bergen's strength had waned, the guard looked at the troll with an evil grin and reached up with one of his large hands to pluck him from the backpack.

Bergen stuck out his tongue and blew a raspberry, before calmly pressing the small button at the end of the handle. The umbrella flew open like a blooming flower. The canopy struck the guard in the side of his head, stunning him. Then the troll lunged forward and poked the guard in the eye with the metal tip. Startled, the soldier released his grip and slid down the metal ladder, taking out the other guards like a bowling ball knocking down pins.

"That's one for the troll," Bergen exclaimed, retracting the umbrella and stashing it back into the knapsack.

"Thanks," muttered Jules, who had been watching over his shoulder.

Jules paused to catch his breath. His heart was pounding. But the danger had passed. "I'm coming," he called up.

He continued his climb. Soon his arms and back ached. He stopped to rest. He felt the metal rung under his feet twist and begin to snap under his weight. Quickly he moved to the next rung and looked down. A fall from this height would kill him. He glanced up; by now Betsy was far above and nearly out of sight. He climbed further, toward the circle of light. Soon he reached the top. He pulled himself over the rim, where he fell onto a bed of soft flowers, exhausted. Betsy was sitting cross-legged on the grass, waiting patiently. It was late morning, and the sun felt good against Jules's skin after all that time in the dark and damp tunnels. He pulled off the backpack and let it fall to the ground. Bergen emerged from a pouch, said something about searching for fresh nuts and berries, and scurried off.

Not far away, Jules noticed a round metal cover in the weeds. He rose, dragged the cover over the top of the silo, and snapped a padlock shut. They were now safe from pursuit.

He pushed the hair out of his eyes and studied the horizon. The snowy peaks still towered over them, but from the west. That could only mean one thing: they had passed completely under the mountains to the other side.

A few feet away, a cool river flowed through a narrow rift in a field of spongy moss. A large nest containing half a dozen orange eggs was half-hidden in the tall grass. The eggs were as big as kickballs. As he watched, one of the eggs began to vibrate, and then a crack appeared along the shell. A narrow head poked out, attached to a long lizard-like neck. The lizard saw Jules, flared its red crest, and hissed.

"Discretion is the better part of valor," Jules said. "Betsy! You better get up. I think we need to get out of here. Those lizards don't look friendly. Why don't we try that way." He pointed to a sign advertising the 'Oasis Resort and Spa.'

"Bergen!" he shouted. "We're leaving!" Moments later the troll reappeared, with red juice dripping down his chin onto his large feet.

They followed a narrow path through a field until they reached a small compound of huts with thatched roofs. Around a bend was a series of refreshment stands and drink bars adjacent to a large swimming pool. A group of giant ants lounged around the pool deck on recliners, sipping colored drinks. The ant-men were tall, taller than Jules, in fact, and had three pairs of limbs. A pair of antennae sprouted from their heads, just above the ears, and swiveled back and forth as if they were trying to pick up radio broadcasts and the reception was spotty.

"Come on," he whispered to Betsy. "Let's get something to drink. And don't stare."

They walked past a trio of ant-men that were constructing a large anthill alongside the edge of the pool. The giant ants glanced at Jules and Betsy, but otherwise showed no reaction to their presence. With their heads down, the children made their way to one of the refreshment stands, which was situated under a large red-and-white striped canopy.

"What will it be, son?" asked the creature behind the counter. She wasn't an ant at all but looked a bit like a pill bug.

"Um . . . I'm not sure." He looked nervously at the selection. "What do you think a person like me might like?"

"Why don't you try one of these?" the bug asked, sliding a roundish piece of dough to him and another to Betsy. "It's a kind of dumpling."

Jules thanked the pill bug, picked up the dumpling and took a bite, half expecting something curious to happen to him as had to Alice whenever she ate food in Wonderland. Instead, he felt full after just a single bite. He took five more of the muffins for future use and stuffed them into his bag. "Aha!" he heard Bergen shout from inside the bag, followed by some faint snacking sounds.

While Jules paid with one of his remaining gold coins, several ant-men approached the counter and ordered sugar cubes and fruity drinks with little umbrellas sticking out of them. "I haven't seen you two at the spa before," said one of the ant-men. He spoke fast and clipped, just as Jules expected a giant ant to sound. The creature took a sip from his drink before continuing. "Are you new here?"

"I guess," Jules said. "We're just passing through."

"You really *are* new here," the ant-man answered.

"Everyone just passes through the spa," said another.

"Where are you headed?" asked a third.

"We're going to Pho Altis," Betsy piped up.

"Pho Altis!" the first ant-man said in that same clipped way. "That's quite a journey."

"Perhaps you should accompany us," said another.

Jules shifted his gaze between them, trying to figure some way to tell them apart. "Oh? Is that where you're headed?"

"Not exactly."

"Close."

"We are on a pilgrimage to the city of Uxita," explained the first ant-man, who seemed to be the most talkative of the group. "It's just on the other side of the Crystal Sea."

"That's only a few days from Pho Altis," added the third.

"For ants."

"We've just stopped here at the spa for a rest."

"It's a dangerous trip."

"Dangerous."

"It's always safer to travel in groups. At least for ants."

The ants all looked at Jules and Betsy awaiting an answer, their antennae shifting back and forth.

"What do you think?" Betsy whispered.

"We'd have to leave right away," Jules said. "I'm late enough as it is."

CHAPTER 13

The Caravan

And so that is how Jules, Betsy, and Bergen found themselves accompanying the band of ant-men on the next leg of their journey. They traveled in a long caravan that stretched for a quarter mile or more, atop large green-and-red animals that seemed a cross between camels and giant lizards. The acabas—which is what the pack animals were called—stood low to the ground on thick legs, and had small, narrow heads at the end of long necks like plant-eating dinosaurs.

Fortunately, the ant-men had several extra acabas used for toting tents and provisions on their expedition, and after a bit of repacking, Jules and Betsy were each provided with their own mounts. Betsy's acaba, they were told, was named Xerxes, while Jules's was called Rumble Butt because of how it swayed while it walked. They sat across the backs of the beasts on long, crusty saddles which looked made from the skin of armadillos sewn together with strips of bark.

They traveled in two parallel rows, following a well-worn path across a wide plain covered by fields of long, golden grass populated by large green moths that flittered about with saucer-shaped wings. Jules and Betsy rode next to each other toward the end of the procession. Bergen went wherever he pleased, at times riding with Jules, at times with Betsy, and at times scampering through the grass.

"I think I'm getting the hang of it," Betsy said, bouncing up and down on the back of her mount. "This is fun."

"Maybe for you," he called back. "My thighs already hurt, and we've been riding for less than an hour."

Betsy frowned. "Haven't you ever ridden a horse?"

"Not counting the wooden ones on a carousel ride? No."

"Well, it's just the same."

"Now that's helpful."

She turned her head. "You're doing it all wrong. You're all tense, and you're not sitting down in the saddle. No wonder you ache."

"I can't sit down all the way. It hurts too much."

"Why don't you take off your jacket for once and use it for extra padding?"

"I would," he replied, "if I could figure out how to stop this giant lizard thing."

Laughing, she steered close and grabbed his reins. A moment later they slowed to a stop.

While Jules folded his jacket into a comfortable seat cover, she said, "My parents made me take riding lessons when I was younger. I hated it. Because I was small I had to ride a mule, and it wouldn't go where it was supposed to. The smell was horrible. These lizard things are much more pleasant."

As they continued their journey, Betsy added, "They just wanted me to learn to do the same things they liked to do. They even made me go to the state fair every year to see the horse riding competition. They never asked me if it was something I wanted to do myself. I always hated that."

"Why didn't you tell them?"

"Tell them? Are you crazy? You've met my parents. They wouldn't say anything, just look at me with a sad look, like I'd failed out of school or set fire to the kitchen. I couldn't handle that."

"Yeah, I know how you feel. Especially about the setting fire to the kitchen part. But I was just seven or eight when I did that, so cut me a break."

"I'm not much older than that, Jules."

"Well, trust me, it's not worth it. A fireman gave me a long talk about being more careful in the future. It hardly caused any damage. I was just trying to make some soup and forgot I had left the burner on, and a dishtowel caught. I don't know what everyone was so upset about."

They came to a rocky ridge, and the two rows of acabas zippered together to proceed single file through a narrow gorge. Steep cliffs rose on either side of the path, with some parts painted in various colors, sometimes with images of animals or nature scenes.

When they were through the canyon, the caravan split back into two rows. The process went slightly amiss, though, and Jules had to let the rider behind him pass so he was once again opposite Betsy.

"What would you do if you could choose?" he asked. "If you hadn't been forced to go horse riding, I mean."

"I don't know. Probably what I'm doing right now."

"Right now? What do you mean?"

"I mean just being on this adventure with you."

"Really?"

"Uh-huh. Since Tarsis, we've done such exciting things. We've ridden bikes, explored caves, hiked. Lots of cool stuff."

"Ridden a train. Don't forget about the train."

Betsy nodded. "Met neat people."

"Ants, you mean."

"Ant-men. And don't forget about those underground gorilla things." She paused, collecting her thoughts. "It's just that—well, when I'm with you, I feel like I can act like myself for once. I don't have to pretend to be someone else or act like I'm at a tea-party with the queen and king, watching my manners and my posture and—and—and, well, not being silly about things. And you listen to me, Jules. No one has ever listened to me before. I mean really listened, not the sort of listening where adults say, 'that's nice, Betsy,' and then go about whatever it was they were doing beforehand."

Jules nodded.

"If I was home right now, I'd probably be running the washing machine or doing math problems in a workbook. It's always one chore after the other."

"Maybe you should tell your parents that."

"Oh, I couldn't do that. I'd be too scared."

"But don't you want to keep doing stuff together when this is all over?"

"Yeah, I do. If they'll let me. I've been having such a great time."

"Me too. I think if you weren't here, I would have given up a long time ago."

"You mean that?"

"Sure I do. I mean, I'm worried crazy about getting my mother back, but having you here has helped somehow."

She blushed slightly. "Thanks."

There was a short silence before Jules asked, "Do you think they're worried about you? Your parents, I mean."

"Probably. We've been gone a long time. I miss them, too. But I feel like I belong with you. You need someone to help you complete your journey, after all. And I think it should be me."

"Thanks, Betsy. I didn't at first, but I do now."

"And I'll see them again when it's all over." She smiled. "I will see them again, right? Just like you'll see your mom again?"

"I think so. But when you do, I think you should tell them what you told me. There's no reason to spend all your time doing stuff that makes you unhappy."

"All they want is what is best for me. I don't want to let them down."

"You have to have a say in your own future." Jules was surprised by his own words, how he was encouraging Betsy to take a stand that he could never do himself. "Only you know what will make you happy. You have to speak up."

Betsy was quiet for a long minute. Then she looked up, her eyes meeting his. "I will if you will." She held out a pinky. "Deal?"

Jules hesitated, then locked fingers. "Deal."

Then she said, "Come on, we're falling behind. We better catch up."

After a time, they reached a point where the golden grass no longer grew. The endless fields were replaced by a harsher environment, dominated by hard rock and packed sand. The sun blazed through a cloudless sky, baking their skin. In the distance, large stone formations thrust up from the ground, like ancient monuments to some past civilization. Wisps of sand and dust blew across the desert floor, reminding Jules of fog on a chilly winter morning.

THE BEAN STORE: THE MAP OF ETERNITY

As they rode, Jules discretely pulled the Map-book from his satchel and flipped it open. By now, he'd become comfortable enough with the swaying of his mount to hold it steady, at least steady enough so he wouldn't get motion sickness from studying the holographic landscape. Due to the bright sun overhead, the image was dim and had a washed-out quality, forcing him to squint until he stumbled upon the brightness and contrast settings hidden inside a recess near the binding. He turned the wheels and things improved.

It didn't take long to locate the snow-capped mountain range under which they had passed while traipsing through the labyrinthine Marochi tunnels. On one side was the green of verdant forest; on the other, a large swath of brown that stretched to the sea. That had to be where they were now. According to the label floating in the air alongside the holographic image, it was known as the Endless Sands.

Jules had heard about the desert, of course, but until now he had never been inside of one, and he realized it was quite different from what was in all the stories. His father had told tales of treks across oceans of sun-bleached dunes in places like Egypt or Mongolia or Arabia, where survival itself depended on the right supplies and luck. But as they rode, he began to notice that the landscape was not as quiet and devoid of life as he would have expected. Plants and bushes sprouted up through the sand and rock, and if he looked hard enough he noticed footprints left by small animals and insects. Sometimes, off in the distance, he saw a half-dozen mud-colored buildings huddled together as if deciding where to go next. As far as he could tell, they had all been long abandoned.

The caravan continued at its slow pace. Betsy held the umbrella over her head to protect her face from the glare, and whenever they felt hungry they snacked on some of the food in Jules's backpack.

They became tired, but the acabas continued forward steadily. Over time Jules and Betsy began to fall farther and farther behind the others, until the rest of the group was just a series of dots along the horizon.

"The desert isn't such a miserable place after all," Jules remarked, breaking the silence and trying to cover the fact he'd been napping in the saddle.

Before Betsy could answer, he noticed a tiny brown spiral cutting across the terrain, bearing down on them from a sharp angle.

"That's curious," he said. "That looks a bit like a—"

"It's a sand storm!" Betsy cried.

"More like a sand tornado," replied Bergen, who was sitting on top of Rumble Butt's head. "Similar to a water spout, except without any water. You see—"

But the rest of the troll's words were lost to the howling wind. Rumble Butt instinctively sat down and lowered his head flat against the ground as a pair of leather flaps extended from behind his ears to cover his eyes and mouth.

"No time to lose," Jules cried. He could barely hear his own voice. Grabbing Bergen, he slipped out of the saddle and slid down his mount's wide backside.

"Betsy!" he screamed as the sand grew thick in the air around him, stinging his cheeks.

"Where are you?" he heard her call back. "I can't see! There's too much sand! What do I do?"

Her voice sounded weak and tiny against the force of the wind. "Get down! Get down on the ground and shut your eyes and cover your face!" He yelled as loud as he could manage, trying to get her to understand, hoping she would hear before it was too late.

But he had to think of his own safety, too. He reached up for his jacket, still folded up as a cushion, and draped it over his head. Then he pulled Bergen tight and whipped his jacket around as cover just as the storm enveloped them. "Betsy!" he cried. "Betsy!" There was no answer as everything around them became dark, the wind rumbling like a passing train. "Oh, Betsy," he whispered. "I wish I could help you."

He huddled against the acaba's bulk, curled in a ball like a centipede that had been frightened. He focused on breathing: in, out, in, out. The noise was everywhere, around him, inside him. The sand pelted him from all directions. He tried not to scream, thought he didn't scream, but heard something that sounded suspiciously like him screaming.

Then, just as suddenly as it had begun, the storm was over. It had lasted no more than a minute. Quiet returned; Jules heard his and Bergen's breathing under the jacket. Whatever had made that screaming sound had stopped. Jules's throat ached from the screaming.

He tried to rise and discovered he was partially buried in sand. He pushed the jacket off, revealing the blue sky. He breathed in the fresh air, felt the sun on his arms and face.

With some effort he stood, opening his eyes. In the distance, the sand tornado zigzagged across the landscape in search of other victims to annoy.

"Well, that wasn't quite so bad," Bergen said as he pulled himself out of the sand and dusted loose particles from his shirt. "I think that could have ended much worse. Don't ya think?"

Jules glanced around in a panic. "Maybe for you and me," he said. "But where's Betsy?"

He felt the blood drain from his face. Her acaba, Xerxes, was only a few yards away, but Betsy had vanished, buried somewhere under the swirling, shifting desert sands. A lump formed deep in his stomach. What could have happened to her? *It's my fault*, he thought. *It's all my fault. She begged me to help her, and all I did was yell.* Now she was lost, but maybe she could be found again, before it was too late. "Xerxes!" he pleaded. "Where is she? Where's Betsy?"

Xerxes stood, shook a layer of sand off her skin, and looked bored.

"It's a dinosaur, boy," Bergen said, rolling his eyes. "It won't answer. It's stupid."

"I'll bet its brain is at least as big as yours," Jules shot back.

"Not when measured as a proportion of body mass," Bergen replied. He pulled out his slide rule and began to say something about troll anatomy, but Jules cut him off with a wave of his hand.

"Not now! Just help me find her before she suffocates!" He turned again to the acaba. "Come on, Xerxes, where is she? Can't you smell her or something? Betsy! Bet-sy!"

Seeming to understand, the acaba swiveled its head and reached out with its long neck, resting it on a mound of sand a few feet away. Jules ran forward to the indicated spot and began digging with his hands at a frenzied pace. He pushed the sand away in large scoops. In seconds he had dug out two, then three feet of the mound. Still there was no sign of her. Not knowing what else to do, he thrust his arm deep into the hole. He felt around, finding nothing but sand. Then his hand touched something solid. He grabbed hold and yanked as hard as he could.

"Gotcha!" he cried, but instead of Betsy he had pulled out an old bone, gleaming white in the bright sun, stripped of its skin and flesh and pockmarked with tiny holes. Jules screamed and dropped it in revulsion and shock.

"Come on, boy," Bergen said, putting away his slide rule and focusing on the problem at hand. "She's still in there. Don't give up."

Jules breathed deep, trying to slow his thumping heart. He tried not to think about what might happen to Betsy if he couldn't locate her. He reached in once again. This time he pulled out a hand—Betsy's hand, from the sight of the blue nail polish. By some luck he had stumbled across her wrist. Now he used both his hands to pull her arm, while Bergen jumped down into the hole and tried to push some more of the sand out of the way with his tiny fingers. Soon the rest of Betsy emerged, gasping and choking, but very much alive.

She sat on a pile of sand, catching her breath. Jules gave her a long hug, and then offered her the cider that Algard and Alesund had packed for him. Betsy took the thermos bottle and took several gulps, nearly choking. She coughed and spit some of it back out onto the hot sand.

"Try some more," Jules pleaded.

This time Betsy was able to keep the liquid down, and soon her breathing returned to normal. "Thanks, Jules," she said in a hoarse whisper once she was able to speak. "I think I'm going to be okay now."

Jules took hold of both her hands and helped her to her feet. He brushed the sand from her hair, her face, her clothes, until she almost looked normal again.

"We better get going," she said, glancing toward the horizon. "We don't want to lose the others."

They remounted and set off in the same direction. After several minutes Bergen located the track the caravan had made through the sand. They urged their acabas forward while it was still light.

Not long afterward they caught up to the ant-men at a small waterhole, where the caravan had stopped for a break.

While waiting for Jules and Betsy, some of the ant-men had built an intricate castle out of the sand. It must've been at least forty feet long, and included doors and turrets. Seeing this, Bergen remarked, "What is it with ants and sand, anyway?" which made Jules laugh.

"Where have you been?" one of the ant-men asked.

"We were—" he started. "Didn't you see the—Why didn't you—?"

He stopped short. The ant-men were looking at him blankly, as if they had no knowledge of what had happened, or they had already forgotten. Jules sighed. It would take too long to explain, and they probably wouldn't care, anyway. They were ants, after all. "It won't happen again," he finally said.

"Make sure it doesn't," the ant-man said sternly, as the sand castle collapsed behind him. "We won't wait again."

CHAPTER 14

The Endless Sands

They remained at the waterhole all night. Betsy swam in the cool water, rubbing her skin to get the remaining sand off her body, while Jules turned away so not to see her without clothes.

The ant-men built a campfire and prepared dinner of roasted meat cooked with maple syrup, since the ants needed to keep their sugar level up.

After dinner, they sang songs and told many stories. They passed around bricks of clay, which they broke off in small pieces and chewed like gum. When it was Jules's turn to provide entertainment, not wishing to disappoint his hosts, he recited an old myth about a hero on an important quest that his father had once told him. Betsy told about the people in the Mayflower who had founded America, which she had done a report on in school during this past year. The ant-men seemed delighted and spent the rest of the night repeating the new stories to each other, memorizing them for future recounting. Their efforts made Jules wonder if any of their stories and songs were original to their culture, or if they were learned from other travelers encountered year after year.

That night he dreamed about his mother.

She was wearing a white gown that was tied across the middle with a sash of blinding sunlight. Her hair had turned cloud-white and fell loosely around her neck as if uncombed. He thought it odd that she wasn't wearing any jewelry: not the golden necklace with the purple stone, not her bracelets, not earrings. He couldn't remember ever seeing her without earrings, and it made her look strange to him, like she was straddling the line between life and death, between being a living, breathing person and a wisp of cloud and memory.

In his dream he sat up in his bed (because he dreamed he was in his old bed), motioned her close. She walked toward him, slowly but with purpose, as if each step gave her pain.

As she grew near, he felt sorrow and worry well up in him, and tears began to flow down his cheeks, unchecked.

She sat on the edge of his bed and wiped the tears with the side of her hand. "Oh my son," she said, "why do you cry?"

"Because I miss you," he blurted.

She stroked his hair. "You're doing fine without me. I can see that, even from this distance."

"How is that possible? I'm here, and you're—you're somewhere else."

She smiled, then took a sip from the teacup that was now in her hand. As she drank, yellow flowers sprouted from her hair, then dropped off onto the floor, where they became vines that slithered across the floor and climbed the walls of his room, enclosing them as if they were in a jail cell. "Never mind that. I'm here now. Is there anything you wish to tell me?"

"I've worked so hard to get to this point," he answered in his heart. "I don't know whether I can go on. Are you alive or dead? I need to know. I need to know that what I'm doing, the hardships I've endured, are for a purpose. That there will be an end to all this, and that we'll be together again soon."

She smiled, a radiant smile that he only remembered from his early childhood. She hadn't smiled like that in—well, for forever. "I am very much alive. I promise you that. And I'm waiting for you to come for me."

"But I have so little strength left." He searched his brain for the right thing to say. "I'm so lonely without you. Betsy is with me, but it isn't the same somehow. I don't know if I can continue. You are so, so very far away."

Once more she smiled, but she didn't say anything. Jules noticed that her skin was crisscrossed with thin dark lines, like someone had drawn on her with a fine point pen. He heard a storm raging outside, wind and rain whipping at the windows. Then she stood and took a step back.

"You are at a crossroads, Jules. Things may get more difficult before they improve. But don't despair. You must have faith—faith that we will both survive, that we will soon see each other again. Hold onto that faith, for within it is a kernel of truth, or at least one possible truth."

"But—"

"Shh. Without faith there is nothing."

All the doubt and indecision that he'd been trying to keep bottled up for the past weeks bubbled up. "I—I don't know how to continue. There are so many decisions to make. What if I mess up? What if I don't make it to you in time?"

His mother looked at him hard, her gaze piercing his very being. "You must trust yourself, and above all, listen to the advice of others who wish to help you. Everyone, no matter how big or small, young or old, has something to offer, either the experience of their own mistakes, or their own untested optimism and intuition. Find those with good hearts, share their wisdom. You will receive help from the unlikeliest of places along your journey."

She pressed something in Jules's hand. He curled his fingers around it, and pulled the thing close to him, not knowing what it was, but feeling that it was important somehow.

His mother smiled again, and in his dream Jules felt a warmth spread through his body, enveloping him like a cocoon. He watched her shrink smaller and smaller, until she vanished.

He opened his eyes. He was lying on the desert floor. The vines were gone. Along the horizon, the sun was starting to rise in the cloudless sky. There was no storm. Next to him, Bergen was stretched on his backpack, snoring softly. His feet started to pump, as if he was running.

"I wonder what trolls dream about," he muttered.

He opened his hand and stared dumbly. In his palm was his mother's necklace, the one with the large purple jewel. Where did it come from? How had she given it to him? He rubbed his thumb across the jewel's smooth surface. He felt a tingle and was engulfed with a feeling of inner peace unlike any he'd had since the start of his journey. He decided not to question this gift. Sitting up, he clasped the chain around his neck, centered it.

Now fully awake, he looked around. The two acabas, Rumble Butt and Xerxes, were huddled together, their legs folded under their bodies. In the other direction slept Betsy, curled in a ball. Jules rose, went to her, and rearranged the blanket so it covered her better. Then he returned to his spot and tried to fall back asleep, thinking of what to say to his mother if she returned to him again.

The caravan traveled in a line across the desert. The ant-men told Jules and Betsy about Uxita, the town where they were headed. They were required to make a pilgrimage there once every seven years, where they could meet with others of their kind and hold a great conference to discuss laws and choose a new leader. "It is the most beautiful town in the world," they told Jules. "It's in the middle of a golden plain, at the junction of three great rivers." In the oldest part of the city, they said, was a stone square known as the Lament, where all sorts of creatures would go and wish for things they had lost.

At one point they rode past a dark spot in the earth, just like the one Jules had seen in the forest. Although smaller, this spot was still about the size of a football field. As before, everything was black inside, even the sand and rock. Once again Jules felt a strange magnetic pull tugging at his muscles. Unable to control his actions, he slipped off his mount and began walking toward it as if possessed, but one of the ant-men reached down and grabbed him by the arm, stopping him. The ant-man's touch broke him of the trance and he regained control of his legs. He backed up until he felt no longer affected by the pull.

The caravan stopped, waiting for Jules to continue their trek.

The black spot seemed to have no effect on Betsy, who had remained atop Xerxes. Yet he had to know what it was, if there was any way to know. The experience had a profound effect on him. How could a physical place turn his willpower to jelly, lead him forward as if his body was a puppet controlled by an invisible puppet master? He turned to the nearest ant-man, who was watching him critically, with the same look a parent has when worried a toddler is about to run into traffic. "What is that place?" Jules asked.

"It's bad luck," was all the ant-man would say.

He grasped the purple stone hanging around his neck and felt a sense of serenity come over him. "Okay. I'll try to stay away in the future."

"Please do."

They made good time across the desert, travelling both day and night, often sleeping on the backs of the acabas as they lumbered across the sand. The acabas had incredible stamina and rarely needed to stop to rest. Jules used the time to catch up in his journal, detailing all the things he had done and seen to this point in his adventure, adding maps and drawings where appropriate.

As they progressed, he discovered that the ant-men were generally a cheerful lot, who enjoyed singing songs and engaging in all sorts of storytelling. They did have one bad habit, however, that Jules first noticed during their stop at the waterhole: a propensity to chew on a thick substance which reminded him of a cross between chewing tobacco and gum. The ant-men carried blocks of it around in their packs, and chewed it constantly, breaking another piece off whenever they ran out.

"Spiggle we call it," said one ant-man, when Jules asked. "Not for kids."

"Addictive," another said.

"But maybe it is okay for humans," a third said.

"Won't know unless you try," said a fourth—or perhaps it was the second speaking again; it was terribly difficult to tell them apart.

"Try," said the closest ant-man. He held out a brick of the stuff with one of his middle pair of feet. "Small amount shouldn't hurt."

"That's small?" Jules muttered, weighing it in his hands. Nervously, he tore off a tiny piece about the size of a jellybean and popped it into his mouth. He bit down, releasing a stream of fizzy bubbles into his mouth. The spiggle had an odd taste, sort of like beer, which his father had once let him drink. He gagged and spit it out into the sand when no one was looking. Catching the eye of one of the ant-men, he quickly smiled and nodded appreciatively. Then, so not to appear rude, he reached down toward his saddle and slipped the rest of the brick into his inner jacket pocket, which he was still using as a cushion—"for later," he said—and thought no more about it.

One day as they were riding, a gentle breeze began to blow from the west, providing unexpected comfort from the brutal daytime heat. Within an hour the breeze strengthened, and the wind blew the sand into the air and against their faces. It stung like needles poking at their skin. Bergen said something about how a desert wasn't fit for trolls, or trolls weren't fit for deserts, and climbed into Jules's backpack for protection, zipping it up behind him.

One of the ant-men turned and pointed at a dark cloud off in the distance, gaining quickly. "A sandstorm comes." It spoke in the short, clipped phrases Jules had become used to. "A big one. They're very dangerous."

The ant-men halted the caravan and briefly conferred among themselves. They spoke in their own language, which sounded like clicks and whirrs, while Jules and Betsy waited nearby, watching the storm grow large as it approached, still miles away.

From his time observing regular-sized ants near his home, he knew they never went off and did anything on their own. They each followed set rules established by the group. He often had marveled at how they followed the same paths once they had been decided upon, making grooves in the dirt like highways from their everlasting traffic. How they came to a decision was something he never understood. Was it the dictate of a leader, the queen ant? Was it through some democratic voting process? Or was it the action of one single daring member of their society, an ant-artist or ant-genius, who experienced a flash of inspiration, and the others followed blindly, followers of their ant-idol? Whatever the case, he realized he was observing this process among the ant-men. Whether it was the same as normal-sized ants he could only speculate.

After a short time, the ant-men seemed to come to a decision. Their antennae started moving around rapidly, as if picking up the brain-waves of the others next to them. Then the antennae all drooped. The clicking sound stopped. The group started to disburse. One of the ant-men scurried on all six legs to where Jules and Betsy were waiting. Then it stood on its lower set of legs to better converse eye-to-eye.

It clicked a few times before switching to English. "We'd better seek cover. There's an old tower nearby. Stone. No one lives there now. We'll be safe there. We better hurry."

The ant-men mounted their acabas and retied their packs tighter. Jules and Betsy ran to climb into their saddles. They spurred the huge lizards forward. The beasts thundered across the desert, raising their own cloud of dust behind them. Without any prompting, Xerxes and Rumble Butt automatically broke into a gallop alongside the others. In moments their speed increased—twenty, thirty, then forty miles per hour, by Jules's estimate. He tightened his grip on the reins and squeezed his thighs against his mount's back, fearful of falling off during this sprint.

The wind whipped at their faces. Jules whooped with glee, as if he was on a theme park ride. Next to him, just a few feet away, Betsy held her reins like a jockey at the races. She had a huge grin on her face, and he could see her laughing, although he couldn't hear anything over the sound of the pounding legs of the acabas around him. Noticing his glance, she took one hand off the reins to wave and flash him the thumbs-up sign. "This is awesome!" she screamed.

Jules nodded emphatically. "I'll bet this is better than anything at some summer camp," he yelled back. He momentarily thought of his classmates from school, wondering what they were doing. Whatever it was, he was sure this topped anything in their lives at that particular instant. For a moment he wished they could see him now—how their opinion of him would change!

That moment was over quickly. Why should he care what they thought of him? He had his own life to lead, making his own memories, his own decisions. And he was with his friend, Betsy, and Bergen too. Betsy, he realized, was the best friend he'd ever had. She followed him unwaveringly and supported him during the one time he needed a friend, when for the first time he had to do things without his mother's help. He didn't need Elmira or the others for affirmation of self-worth. One good friend, he realized, was worth far more than the opinions of two dozen classmates who mocked and laughed at him. He looked over at Betsy again and returned the thumbs-up gesture.

Betsy nodded and waved, laughing. Then she seemed startled by something, and looked behind, frowning. "It's not just a sandstorm," she yelled to him. "It's Alexis, too. She's coming back."

He twisted his body, but saw only the dark cloud, now closer than ever. He shook his head. "I don't—"

Betsy interrupted him. "I can hear her calling over the wind. Can't you hear her?"

Jules shut his eyes and listened. Over the top of the howling wind he could just make out a light buzzing sound. He twisted around again. The sandstorm was almost on top of them. Then, flying ahead of the approaching storm, he once again saw the form of the beautiful woman, edges blurred as component parts moved in and out of position. Her arms were outstretched toward him. "I have come for the Map," he heard her call. "The Map! Give it to me, Jules, and I won't hurt you."

"Let's get out of here!" Jules screamed. He kicked his heels into Rumble Butt's back and tugged on the reins. Rumble Butt correctly interpreted what Jules wanted it to do and shifted into a higher gear. The sudden acceleration pushed Jules back in the saddle. The other animals in the caravan, sensing the urgency, matched this new pace, remaining in tight formation. Jules leaned precariously over his mount's neck, as if he could urge it forward with his thoughts alone.

Still, though, Alexis and the sandstorm gained. The sand swirled around Jules's head, pelting his bare skin. He narrowed his eyes to tiny slits and covered them with one of his hands, looking through the gaps between his fingers, trying to protect them from the powerful wind and stinging grains of sand.

"Let me come to you," Alexis's voice called. "My touch will soothe your skin, take away the hurt. Let me heal your pain."

He ignored these advances and pushed Rumble Butt harder, faster. Then, up ahead, he saw a tower rising from the desert floor, broken in parts, possibly all that remained of a once-great castle long eroded by the fickle desert sands. The ant-men adjusted their direction, and now the caravan was heading directly toward the structure, still at full gallop. Jules could hardly see from all the sand whipping around his face.

They rushed through the front gate of a stone wall, through a courtyard, and into an inner hall of the tower itself just as the storm overtook them, filling the air with sand that darkened the sky. As the ant-men shut the large wooden door, barring it, Jules heard the swarm of insects tearing away at the stone and rock, breaking it down, piece by piece, shard by shard, just as they had done to the town of Tarsis. Alexis screamed and the wind howled. The tower trembled under the pressure of the storm and the fury of the swarm.

Jules and Betsy huddled together in the corner, far from the doorway. Bergen left the safety of the backpack and sat with his friends, facing the danger in the same way. Jules thought about his mother and prayed that they weren't going to die here in the desert, that he'd be able to see her again. He heard bricks crash to the ground outside the tower. Or perhaps it was the sound of stone thrown against the tower wall, to break it apart. Who could tell in the maelstrom of such fury, of such malice?

Jules grabbed the purple jewel hanging around his neck, and once again felt a sense of serenity come over him. Next to him, Betsy was trembling with fear. Without knowing why, he unclasped the necklace and connected it around her neck. "For luck," was all he said.

A crack opened in the wall, and a thin line of insects streamed through. Betsy screamed as they tried to coalesce into a new form, something to cause mischief and pain and destruction.

"Here we go," said Bergen, adopting a fighting pose.

But they had forgotten about the acabas, standing idly in the center of the tower floor. As the insects began to swarm, began to morph into this new form, the giant lizards reached out with their long necks and plucked them from the air with their mouths, eating them before the insects could cause any trouble.

The buzz became high-pitched, either an expression of pain or a warning to the rest of the swarm to stay away, that there was danger in the tower, that it was a trap. The acabas chewed, and goo oozed down their chins and dripped onto the stone floor. The insects, furious, darted in and out of range, trying to set upon the acabas and sting them in the eyes, the tongue, anywhere that might be sensitive enough to get these horrible beasts to slink away, to leave them alone.

Bergen yanked on Jules's pants leg. "Yer better close up that crack while they're distracted," the troll suggested.

"Good idea."

As the battle raged just above their heads, Jules scooped a handful of mud and dirt from the ground and packed it into the crevice, pressing hard with his fingers until it was sealed shut, preventing the entry of any more of the insects.

Then it was over. The last of the swarm inside the tower had been eaten, destroyed.

The ant-men sat in a circle and sang songs, not paying any attention to the storm swirling outside the tower, as if this was no different from any other day in their lives, and they had just stopped here for a short rest. Gradually, though, the wind stopped and all became quiet. The ant-men opened the door and peered out. The storm was gone; the sky was clear and blue. Of Alexis there was no sign.

"Maybe the storm drove her away," Betsy said.

"She'll be back," Jules warned as he stepped out into the sunshine. "I'm sure of it. But it seems as if we're safe for now."

"Well, well, what a wonderful day," said one of the ant-men, already having forgotten about the storm, and never being aware of Alexis in the first place. "Let's continue on. We still have so far to go."

Jules's adventure concludes in
Book Two of *The Bean Store*, titled
The Crystal Sea.

ABOUT THE AUTHOR

After growing up in New Jersey, Warren Firschein graduated from the University of Rochester in 1989 with a degree in political science, followed by a law degree from the University of Pittsburgh and an MBA from Carnegie Mellon University. He is the author of two previous middle-grade novels, *The Pirate of Janaconda Island* (Chapter Two Press, 2017) and *Out of Synch* (Chapter Two Press, 2015), considered the all-time best-selling middle grade novel about the sport of synchronized swimming. In addition, he is the coauthor (with Laura Kepner) of *A Brief History of Safety Harbor, Florida* (History Press, 2013). More recently, he is the cofounder and managing editor of *Odet*, a Florida-based literary journal. When not writing, he is an attorney for the Federal Communications Commission. He lives in Florida with his wife, Dawn, and their two daughters, Sophie and Elena. Visit him at www.warrenfirschein.com.